The Bookshop

a play in two acts

Performance Edition

by

Jamie Lambdin-Bolin

This playscript is a work of fiction. Any names of characters, businesses or places, or events or incidents are fictitious. Any resemblance to actual persons, living or dead, or actual events is purely coincidental.

The Bookshop was originally self-published in 2023. This updated version includes cast and crew information from the original staged production.

The Bookshop is a companion to *Coffee Shop*, also written by Jamie Lambdin, or Jamie Lambdin-Bolin. The stories are independent of each other but take place within the same literary or theatric universe.

Edited by Marcus Coker

Character Descriptions

THE BOOKSHOP. A sort of character in and of itself. A popular local haunt for book lovers, students, and more. The place carries an almost accidental whimsy to it and is home to books old and new. Above the bookshop is a sort of housing quarters, where Rae, the owner, lives with her husband.

RAE MARCH. Female. 30s. Bookshop owner. Loves books. Maintains a playful relationship with her customers and employees. Currently trying to get pregnant.

CHARLIE. Written as female; gender can depend on the person playing the role. 20s. Witty and curious.

JEREMY. Male. Mid to late 20s. Athletic. Competitive. A bit clingy.

PETER LOCHLAN. Male. 30s. Close friends
with Rae and Calvin. A bestselling author
under his pen name, Colson Graves.

CALVIN MARCH. Male. 30s to 40s. Rae's
husband. Supportive but not overbearing;
busy but laidback. Music director at the
local Presbyterian church.

DOUGLAS WAYNE. Male. Mid 50s+. Quirky.
Frequent customer and avid reader.

DOTTY JONES. Female. 50s+. Another
customer at the bookstore. A bit of a
pain, but with a good heart.

CASSIE. Female. 40s to 50s. Yoga instructor
and customer. A bubbly personality.

BARRIE. Bookstore cat famous in Fort Smith.
Casting optional.

VARIOUS CUSTOMERS.

Original Cast

Performed in October 2024 at Bookish: An Indie Shop
for Folks Who Read
Fort Smith, Arkansas

RAE... Monica Longoria
CHARLIE... Taylor Newby
JEREMY…………………………….…….. Logan Davis
PETER…………………………………….….. Eric Wells
CALVIN……………………………………… Brandon Bolin
DOUGLAS………………………………….. Kurt Marine
DOTTY……………………………………….Micki Voelkel
CASSIE……………….……………… Shannon Stoddard
BARRIE…………………………………………. Herself

Note: The script includes space for an ensemble cast.
Ensemble lines were provided to named characters in
the original production but remain in this edition as
ensemble lines.

CONSULTING
Cody Banning; Kim and Rusty Peoples; Audra Sargent
and Charles Belt; Juno, Sylvie, CJ, and CB, Markus
Coker

Special thanks to Sara Putman for partnering with me to
use Bookish as our first performance venue and turn a
stage play into an immersive theatre experience. And for
being *really* nice since, like, 2013 about my writing.

Contents

SETTING

Rae's Bookshop, present-day in October

ACT ONE

Scene One: "Put It on the Sandwich Board"
Scene Two: "Busy Doing What?"
Scene Three: "Advance Copy"
Scene Four: "Coffee, No Coffee"

ACT TWO

Scene One: "I Saw It at Gale's"
Scene Two: "I Wonder Who It's From"
Scene Three: "Mr. Graves"
Scene Four: "I Miss Everything"

ACT ONE

SCENE 1
"Put It on The Sandwich Board"

(At rise: LIGHTS COME UP on a friendly bookstore with worn-ish-looking walls, shelving, and a wooden floor. On the Far Right Wall, a sign that lists genres and is pointing offstage. On the Far Left Wall, an EXIT sign and an arrow pointing off left. Along the walls, local art hangs. Comfortable couches and chairs as well as the odd display table throughout. Upstage, somewhere left of center, a checkout counter. Near, a staircase leads to the upstairs living quarters. Customers browse shelves or are seated with their selections. Somewhere visible, a handwritten sign on a stand reads "LOCAL AUTHOR MEET & GREET @ 4:30." DSL, a customer whom we will soon know as DOUGLAS is seated in a chair with a large stack of books piled on the floor in front of him. CHARLIE is talking to him. JEREMY is in the process

*of pretending to be dusting shelves. He is
absent-minded, staring into space.*

Barrie, the shop cat, lurks nearby.)

CHARLIE. Douglas. We've talked about this.
You can't just leave books on the floor.

DOUGLAS. I'm not just leaving the books. I
might want to buy them.

CHARLIE. What happens when Rae walks by
and sees this mess? *(DOUGLAS
shrugs.)* I'm serious. Every time you
come in here you pile all these books up
all over the place, and I get in trouble
because I let you get the covers dirty.

DOUGLAS. Maybe you should do a better job
of cleaning then.

CHARLIE. Douglas. *(Nearby, a CUSTOMER
shushes them.)* Sorry. *(Quieter)* Doug.
Please. You've gotta help me out here.

DOUGLAS. All right. Let me start with these *(gathering a few)*.

CHARLIE. *(Accepting them)* Thank you. I'll put these on the counter for you. Are there any others you're thinking about?

DOUGLAS. *(Thinking)* Well … No. No, I think you can shelve them. I will be back, after all *(Chuckling to himself and patting his pockets)*. You know, I think I left my wallet in the car. Let me go get it.

CHARLIE. Sure.

(DOUGLAS exits, and CHARLIE makes her way to JEREMY, quietly.)

CHARLIE. Do you know you've been dusting the same spot for like five minutes?

JEREMY. No, I haven't.

CHARLIE. I'm just saying. *(He makes a face.)* What?

JEREMY. I didn't say anything.

CHARLIE. Okay. *(She turns to move away
     again. He sighs again.)* Jeremy, *what* are
     you doing? *(A CUSTOMER shushes
     them.)* Sorry *(To JEREMY. Quieter).*

JEREMY. I'm rearranging the display table that
     you messed up. Cleaning up your *mess.*

CHARLIE. Oh, whatever.

JEREMY. I do that a lot, you know.

CHARLIE. *(Mimicking)* "I do that a lot, you
     know." *(Sliding a book off the table; the
     book crashes to the floor)* Oops. Guess
     you'll have to clean that up too. *(She
     moves away, retreating toward the
     checkout counter where a CUSTOMER
     has now rung the bell on the counter
     twice.)* Sorry about that.

*(RAE enters through the door behind the
     checkout counter. She carries a box of*

*books. She comes downstage to an
empty table and sets the box down.)*

RAE. Jeremy, can you give me a hand with
these?

JEREMY. *(Approaching, he drops the feather
duster he's been carrying onto a nearby
chair.)* Sure. *(They begin unpacking the
books, organizing them into small stacks
on the table.)*

*(DOTTY, another customer, appears. She
makes a disapproving noise.)*

DOTTY. Just as I thought. More fornication.

JEREMY. Excuse me?

DOTTY. Rae Ellen, why must you slight the
Lord?

RAE. Oh. *(Turning her attention back to the
books more than the conversation)* I don't
know … Old habit I guess.

JEREMY. *(To DOTTY)* Did you say—

DOTTY. It is not wise to make jokes about sin,
    Rae Ellen. Your shelves are stuffed to the
    rafters with fornication. And scantily clad
    women.

RAE. You're welcome to take one home since
    you find them so interesting.

JEREMY. That's just the erotica portion of our
    romance section, Mrs. Jones. We have
    plenty of other genres to choose from
    that should suit your preferences.

DOTTY. *(Ignoring this statement)* I am talking
    about breasts, Rae Ellen.

RAE. I'm sorry, I've not heard of those. Could
    you describe them to me?

DOTTY. Very funny.

RAE. Dotty, I appreciate your business and I
    would never want to dissuade you from
    visiting our store, but I'm afraid we have

more books in the romance genre than we do Bibles or even classic literature. I've been to at least seventy used bookstores, and they're all generally the same in that aspect. Apparently, erotica is very popular. It's right up there next to murder mysteries and Westerns.

(DOTTY makes a "hmph" noise and begins to make her way to the door, through which PETER has just entered).

PETER. Oh, excuse me.

DOTTY. *(To herself. Emphatically)* Sexual relations are a private matter and should not be displayed on store shelves for the public to see.

PETER. I'm sorry?

DOTTY. *(Turning back to RAE across the room)* It isn't decent, Rae Ellen!

RAE. Bye, Dot!

(DOTTY exits.)

RAE. Jeremy?

JEREMY. Yes?

RAE. I want you to start on a sign. For the rest
    of the month, used erotic novels are
    twenty percent off.

JEREMY. Okay.

RAE. And Jeremy?

JEREMY. Yes?

RAE. Make sure you put that on the sandwich
    board before you put it on the sidewalk
    tomorrow morning.

(JEREMY leaves to do as he's been told.)

RAE. *(Catching sight of the books on the floor)*
    Charlie?

CHARLIE. Yes?

RAE. Books on the floor.

CHARLIE. Dang it.

(CHARLIE crosses downstage to retrieve the pile. DOUGLAS has reentered by now and is making his way to the counter. He rings the bell.)

RAE. Good afternoon, Douglas *(Crossing behind the counter)*.

DOUGLAS. Afternoon, Miss Rae.

RAE. Find anything special today?

DOUGLAS. That pile there belongs to me.

RAE. Wonderful. And does that pile belong to you as well *(Acknowledging the mess downstage)?*

DOUGLAS. You caught me.

RAE. I'm going to charge you extra if you keep
     leaving my store like that.

DOUGLAS. Aw, now. You don't really mean
     that.

RAE. Try me.

DOUGLAS. *(Holding his hands up in surrender)*
     Point taken. I'll mind my manners from
     now on.

RAE. Thank you.

DOUGLAS. Give me just a few minutes to
     make up my mind on some of those
     others, and I'll be back to check out. How
     does that sound?

RAE. *(A warm smile)* That's fine.

(PETER stops CHARLIE, *who was just walking
     past him on her way to another area of
     the store).*

PETER. Excuse me?

CHARLIE. What's up?

PETER. Do you work here?

CHARLIE. Yeah *(Exits).*

PETER. … Okay.

RAE. Jeremy, you've got five minutes.

JEREMY. *(Offstage)* I know.

RAE. Are you ready?

JEREMY. *(Reentering)* Yes.

RAE. Got your books?

JEREMY. Yeah.

RAE. Got something to write with? Is your table
	set up?

JEREMY. Yeah.

RAE. Okay. Where is everything?

JEREMY. What do you mean? Oh! *(He bolts offstage.)*

PETER. Rae!

RAE. Peter! *(They hug.)* You look good.

PETER. You look old.

RAE. *(Giving him a pinch)* Hey.

PETER. Only joking.

RAE. Maybe I'll need to reconsider this thing.

PETER. I'm already here. You wouldn't send me away, would you?

RAE. I don't guess so.

PETER. Is Calvin around?

RAE. Should be soon.

PETER. And will you two be sharing any news
    with me today?

RAE. *(Holding up her left hand)* Not yet. Sorry
    to disappoint.

PETER. Darn. I thought for sure when you
    called me that it had happened.

RAE. Patience, patience. Jeesh. You sound just
    like Calvin.

PETER. Can you blame me? My girl's going to
    have a baby—

RAE. *(Loudly)* Hush! *(She is joined by a chorus
    of "shh" noises from CUSTOMERS
    nearby.)* Sorry. *(Back to PETER)* We're
    sort of keeping that to ourselves for now.

PETER. Really? Why?

RAE. Well, this is a small town. Gossip travels
    quickly, and I'd rather *I* found out about
    my pregnancy before everyone else
    does.

PETER. Right. Right. Sorry. *(Pulling her in for another hug)* Don't worry. My lips are sealed.

RAE. Thank you.

(JEREMY reenters, carrying a fold-down table. CHARLIE follows close behind, carrying a large box).

JEREMY. Table. Check. Books and pens?

CHARLIE. Check check.

(They begin setup.)

PETER. Is this the team?

RAE. Yup. This is them.

CHARLIE. You can't stack them like that, they'll fall over.

JEREMY. *(Mimicking her)* You can't stack them like that, they'll fall over.

CHARLIE. Fine then. Have it your way.

JEREMY. Fine then, have it your way. *(Not paying attention at all to what he's doing, he knocks a stack of books down.)*

RAE. *(To PETER)* I don't know if I'd call it a team. Jeremy, Charlie, this is Peter.

JEREMY/CHARLIE. Hello/Hey.

RAE. Peter's an old friend. He'll be around for a few weeks, so you might see him around the shop.

PETER. I'll try not to be in the way too much.

CHARLIE. Must be some vacation plan, spending three weeks in a town like this.

PETER. Erm, well. I guess I'm here mostly for work. Catch up with friends. You know.

JEREMY. Are you from here?

RAE. He sure is. Coming home for a visit and
    to get some writing done.

CHARLIE. You're a writer?

PETER. In a way.

JEREMY. What was your name, again?

PETER. Peter Lochlan. Nice to meet you
        (Attempting to initiate a handshake).

JEREMY. *(Accepting his outstretched hand
        before returning to his mess)* Never
        heard of you.

PETER. Well, I guess you wouldn't have. I
        mostly do, uh—

RAE. Freelance. Copywriting for different
        companies.

PETER. Articles, some ghostwriting *(Reaching
        his outstretched hand toward CHARLIE).*

RAE. Right.

CHARLIE. *(Ignoring his attempted handshake)*
How does that work?

PETER. *(He retrieves his hand.)* There's an
app. Companies post jobs. I pick them
up.

JEREMY. *(His interest is piqued.)* And you
make good money doing that?

PETER. Sure.

CHARLIE. So you came here to do freelance
copywriting?

PETER. Among other things.

*(His books restacked, JEREMY clears his voice
pointedly).*

RAE. Jeremy here is a writer, too.

PETER. Really? Oh. I see. *(He picks up a copy
of Jeremy's book.)*

JEREMY. It's nothing, really. Just some hiking guides.

PETER. Useful.

JEREMY. It won an award.

PETER. Really? That's great.

CHARLIE. Just the local Parks and Recreation seal of approval. Not really what I call an award.

(JEREMY makes a face at her. Then, the door opens, and CALVIN enters. He holds a large box in his arms).

CALVIN. Delivery. *(He crosses toward the counter. RAE & PETER meet him there. JEREMY and CHARLIE remain behind, bickering.)*

PETER. Calvin, good to see you.

CALVIN. *(Nodding, with a smile)* Peter. *(A little quieter)* I bet it'll be even better to see what just came in.

PETER. Already?

RAE. Should be. Let's open it. *(She grabs a pair of scissors and begins cutting into the tape on the box.)*

PETER. Good timing.

RAE. This is so exciting! *(Pulling out a small stack and proudly handing one to PETER before passing one to CALVIN)* They Found Her on Sixth Street *by Colson Graves!* "Do not open before October 31."

CALVIN. *(Reading the back cover)* "A chilling tale of love and murder. Gripping. You won't be able to put it down." *(To PETER)* High praise!

RAE. "The resolution is so sickening, I couldn't sleep for a week."

CHARLIE. *(Unnoticed, she has approached behind them.)* Is that the new Colson Graves book?

RAE. Yup!

CHARLIE. Can I see?

RAE. *(Handing her a copy)* Sure. But you know the rules—

CHARLIE. No opening until the release date. I know.

CALVIN. It is tempting.

RAE. I thought I gave you my advanced copy.

CALVIN. You did.

RAE. Then where is it?

CALVIN. Erm ...

RAE. You lost it?

CALVIN. So? My wife owns the store. Can't I just have a copy? (She gives him a look.) Can't I just buy a copy?

RAE. Well, I guess, but I was kind of hoping to read it before the release date.

CALVIN. Read one of the finished copies.

RAE. I want to save those for the release date. It's more fun this way.

PETER. *(He has noticed CHARLIE, deeply engrossed in inspecting the cover, specifically the author's bio.)* Are you a fan?

CHARLIE. Sure. He's so good at writing mysteries … horrifyingly good. Usually.

PETER. Usually?

CHARLIE. Well … *(A guilty look in CALVIN's direction)* I may have read it already.

RAE. Advanced copy?

CHARLIE. It was on top of the cash register.

RAE. And where is it now?

CHARLIE. I left it on your kitchen counter, like,
      a week ago.

RAE. Oh.

PETER. What did you mean by "usually"? Did
      you not like the book?

CHARLIE. I mean, I liked it—

PETER. But you didn't love it.

CHARLIE. I've read the story somewhere else.

RAE. Somewhere else?

CHARLIE. The girl is found murdered in the
      bank of a small, sleepy town the day after
      Halloween. They arrest her boyfriend, but
      it's not actually him, so they have to let

him go. I mean I love his books, usually.
But I've read the story somewhere
before. It's been done.

PETER. It's been *done?*

CHARLIE. Maybe I read too many mysteries.

CALVIN. Sure. I mean, how many ways can
you murder a character before the stories
start to repeat a little?

RAE. Charlie, can you store these in my office?

CHARLIE. Sure. *(She exits with the box.)*

PETER. *(To CALVIN)* Repeat a little, Cal?

CALVIN. Sorry. I didn't mean it like that.

PETER. *(Shocked) They Found Her on Sixth
Street* is an original story!

RAE and VARIOUS CUSTOMERS. *Shhh!*

PETER. *Sorry.*

CASSIE. Excuse me.

RAE. Yes, how can I help you?

CASSIE. *(Smiling broadly)* I'm Cassie and I'm
new here—well, not new to town. I've
lived here all my life. But I'm opening a
yoga studio right on the corner of Fourth
and Main and I was wondering if I could
bring some cards by?

RAE. *(Alarmed)* Fourth and Main? Not where
the donut shop is, I hope.

CASSIE. Oh, no. The other side of the street.

RAE. Oh. Thank God. If that place goes, so do
I.

CASSIE. They do make the very best maple
bars.

RAE. Agreed. Anyway, sorry. Yes, I would love
to take some cards.

CHARLIE. *(Reentering)* I just ended up putting the box on the floor. Is that okay?

RAE. Sure.

CASSIE. I'll get outta your hair. Thanks, Rae! Nice to meet you all. *(She walks to exit the store.)*

RAE. You too! *(After she's gone, to PETER and CALVIN)* How about we talk about lunch in the office?

CHARLIE. If you can all fit in there. It's kind of a mess.

RAE. Thank you, Charlie.

(RAE, PETER, and CALVIN exit. CHARLIE leans on the counter, deep in thought.)

At some point during the above action, DOTTY made her way back into the store. She has spent some time at JEREMY's elbow getting him to sign a copy of his book for

*her. Now, she has made her way to the
checkout counter.)*

DOTTY. Excuse me!

CHARLIE. *(Startled, she comes out of her
reverie.)* Oh. Yes?

DOTTY. Well? Aren't you going to ring me up?

CHARLIE. Oh. Yes.

DOTTY. Then hadn't you better *do* it?

CHARLIE. Sorry. *(She tries to share a knowing
smile.)* I was thinking about a book I just
finished reading.

DOTTY. *(She either does not catch or does not
care for, the book-loving camaraderie
CHARLIE has tried to share with her. She
simply begins the process of digging
through her purse to find her billfold.
Some of the items she retrieves are
normal, like a box of mints, but the final
object she removes before her billfold is*

a pistol in a case.) Well, do it later, when you're not on the clock! Don't you know it's disrespectful to keep your customers waiting while you stand there with your head in the clouds like a dolt?

CHARLIE. *(A little annoyed, she takes the book and begins to ring her up, and also eyes the gun.)* I'm sorry. I didn't mean to make you wait.

DOTTY. Well, you have. *(She notices CHARLIE looking at the gun.)* What're you staring at? You wanna see my permit?

CHARLIE. Uh. No, I'm good. That'll be $16.41.

DOTTY. *(Passing her credit card)* I ought to have a talk with Rae Ellen about proper employee behavior.

DOUGLAS. *(Politely)* Excuse me? *(He stands behind DOTTY, holding a large pile of books in his arms.)*

DOTTY. Wait your turn.

(By now, RAE, PETER, and CALVIN have reentered from the office).

RAE. Dot. Back so soon?

DOTTY. *(Very seriously and while repacking her purse)* Well, of course. We *must* support our local authors. *(To CALVIN)* Calvin, I'll see you tonight at choir practice.

CALVIN. I'll see you then!

(DOUGLAS reenters. He has a pleasant reaction as he sees and recognizes PETER.)

RAE. Thank you for your patronage.

CHARLIE. *(Her hand extended)* Here's your receipt.

DOTTY. Hmph! *(She stalks away and exits through the shop door).*

CALVIN. Goodness. What was that about?

DOUGLAS. (*Setting his books on the counter*)
    The sun doesn't need a reason to shine.
    Dorothy Jones doesn't need a reason to
    work herself into a tizzy. (*To PETER*)
    Hello there, young man!

PETER. Hello.

RAE. Wise words, Doug. Well, what did you
    decide?

DOUGLAS. I'll take 'em all.

(*LIGHTS OUT.*)

SCENE 2
"Busy Doing What?"

(Scene: Late afternoon; the store is closed, and all customers and employees are gone for the day. CALVIN stands downstage next to a music stand. He is humming while he looks through music in a binder. RAE enters from the upstairs apartment. She wears a thick robe and slippers.)

RAE. Cal, what are you doing?

CALVIN. Setting things up, darling.

RAE. For what?

CALVIN. Rehearsal.

RAE. It's the third of October.

CALVIN. You said you wanted Christmas carols in the shop this year. These things take a little time.

RAE. You need two months of rehearsal for one afternoon of caroling?

CALVIN. Well, darling, with one rehearsal a week …

RAE. I know … But babe. *(She gestures to her ensemble.)*

CALVIN. Hm?

RAE. We had plans tonight.

CALVIN. I asked you if we were busy tonight, and you said we needed to be planning for the Immaculate Conception.

RAE. No. I said at the rate things have been going, I should be praying for an Immaculate Conception. *(She slips one shoulder out of the robe.)*

CALVIN. Oh. You mean our baby.

RAE. Yes, dear.

CALVIN. Well, I'm going to be busy here for
    about an hour.

RAE. *(Dropping the robe off her other shoulder,
    revealing the top of the negligee
    underneath)* Busy with what?

CALVIN. I told you. *(He turns, spotting her.)* Oh.

RAE. Mhmmm. *(She descends from the
    countertop and starts moving toward
    him.)*

CALVIN. W-well. I-I ... *(She reaches him and
    unties her robe, letting it fall to the
    ground.)* I suppose we could p-postpone
    rehearsals.

RAE. Good idea. *(She places her hands on his
    shoulders. He pulls her to him. They
    remain here for a moment as he kisses
    her neck).*

CALVIN. Have I told you lately how exceedingly
    beautiful you are?

RAE. I could stand to hear it again.

CALVIN. *(A thought occurs to him.)* You know,
	speaking of Immaculate Conception …

RAE. Hmm.

CALVIN. Well, I thought you were talking about
	Christmas.

RAE. Mhm.

CALVIN. But you know, I don't think the
	Immaculate Conception refers to Jesus.

RAE. It doesn't?

CALVIN. No. I think it refers to Mary.

RAE. Cal.

CALVIN. Yes?

RAE. Can we maybe stop talking about Mary
	and Jesus for a minute?

CALVIN. Oh. Yes. Right. *(He kisses her.)*

*(A loud rapping noise comes from the Front
Door.)*

VOICE. Ding dong! Here we come
a-wassailing!

RAE. Your carolers are here.

CALVIN. Ignore them. Maybe they'll go away.

(A beat before RAP RAP, from the front door.)

DOTTY's VOICE. All ye faithful … Come open
the door! *(RAP RAP RAP)*

RAE. Is that Dotty?

CALVIN. Hm.

RAE. Maybe you should …

CALVIN. Hm?

DOTTY. Rae Ellen — let us in!

RAE. *(Leaning away from her husband)* That's one way to kill the mood.

CALVIN. I don't guess I can reasonably ask them to go now.

RAE. No.

CALVIN. Maybe later we can …

DOTTY. Calvin Louis, I know you're in there!

CALVIN. *On my way! (He sighs.)* You'd better get upstairs if you want to avoid being seen like that. *(Giving his best DOTTY impression)* It isn't decent!

RAE. All the better for her. Since when does she carol anyway?

CALVIN. I think I recall someone telling her to get out more.

RAE. What jerk gave her that idea?

CALVIN. If only we knew. *(She laughs and exits upstairs as he opens the door.)*

DOTTY. *(Enters along with three others)* Finally.

CALVIN. Are these all the volunteers we have? I counted at least ten.

SINGER. They went home. *(Shoots a pointed look at DOTTY)*

CALVIN. Oh. Well, if you'll just gather near the sofa.

SINGER 2. What are we singing?

CALVIN. Wait, I've got binders. *(He goes to glance behind the counter.)*

SINGER 3. I hope we do "Mary, Did You Know?". I love that song.

DOTTY. It's the stupidest religious Christmas carol.

SINGER 1. I wouldn't say it's stupid.

DOTTY. What was the point of sending angels
to tell the girl, then?

SINGER 2. Calvin, do you think it's a stupid
song?

CALVIN. *(Rising from the counter)* Maybe
upstairs? *(He begins crossing.)*

SINGER 3. Are you going to tell us what you
think, Calvin?

CALVIN. *(Having made it to the top of the stairs
and pausing to look back at them)* I have
it on good authority that, at least some of
it, Mary did know. And that does kind of
… mess with the point of the song a little.

*(The door at the top of the stairs opens, and
RAE, still in her negligee, hands CALVIN
a stack of binders. SINGERS bicker
unaware).*

DOTTY. I told you.

SINGER. You suck all the fun out of everything.

CALVIN. Okay! *(Returning to the ground floor)* Now I know we're starting this process a bit early, but I was hoping that we'd have some caroling in shifts throughout December. And considering that December is my, well, busy time, I thought it would be best to over-prepare rather than—

(He is interrupted by a knock at the door.)

CALVIN. Just a moment. *(Headed toward the door)* It looks like we may have more singers after all. *(Upon opening the door)* Oh. Hi, Jeremy.

JEREMY. Hey! *(Looking in)* What's going on?

CALVIN. Rehearsal.

JEREMY. Oh *(Not moving from the entry.)*

CALVIN. You want to join us?

JEREMY. Oh. No.

CALVIN. Okay. Are you coming in, or … ?

JEREMY. Could I?

CALVIN. Well, not to be rude, but I kind of need
to get back to this.

JEREMY. I mean I guess I could come in. Read
a book or something. Ha.

CALVIN. Great. *(Closing the door)* Okay. Where
were we?

SINGER 1. December is your busy time.

CALVIN. Right. So, I want to get as much done
ahead of time, as … Jeremy, what are
you doing?

JEREMY. *(Who has tucked himself behind the
checkout counter and is moving books,
notebooks, and other items around)* Uh.
Looking for a book.

(During the following, JEREMY makes his way up the stairs toward the residential door and exits.)

CALVIN. Okay. Anyway, I wanted to frontload our practice so that when December gets here, you'll only need me to conduct. If you'll look at the music I've provided—

DOTTY. Calvin, are these secular songs?

CALVIN. Um. Well—

DOTTY. I wasn't aware we'd be singing secular music during the most important Christian holiday of the year.

CALVIN. All things considered, I was hoping for a lighthearted, more inclusive feel.

SINGER 2. Play nice, Dot. Or the other kids won't want to sing with you.

(JEREMY reappears on the landing. Embarrassed, he descends the stairs.)

SINGER 3. Going to join us, Jeremy?

JEREMY. Oh, no. I'm not great at singing.

CALVIN. You're welcome to sing along. It's all
          in good fun, anyway.

JEREMY. No, that's okay. I got what I came for
          (carrying a book toward the front door).
          See you guys tomorrow. (Exits)

SINGER 2. *(To DOTTY)* See what I mean?

CALVIN. All right, without further ado, let's turn
          to the first printout in your binders—

SINGER 1. Can I go to the bathroom first?

CALVIN. *(Looking a bit defeated)* Of course.
          Let's take five.

(SINGER 1 exits.

LIGHTS OUT.)

SCENE 3

"Advance Copy"

*(The next day, late afternoon. The Book House
hosts a small crowd. Some customers
wander the aisles, while some sit with a
book or two.*

*Near center stage, DOTTY and RAE are
arranging chairs for what looks like a
book club meeting. DOTTY is getting on
RAE's last nerve. RAE is dressed for a
date, including bright red lips.*

*JEREMY is perched behind the checkout
counter, his nose deep in a book, which
he has almost finished. CHARLIE brings
more chairs out of a closet, passing him
as she goes.)*

CHARLIE. Psst. *(He does not respond, only
sticks a finger up in her direction to signal
"Give me one minute.")* Are you almost
done?

DOTTY. *(A mite impatiently)* Don't you have
any tables we could use? This is a Bible
study. We can't likely take notes on our
laps, can we?

RAE. *(Who, under the previous line, has been
taking a moment to smooth her skirt and
offerering the older woman a
mostly-patient smile)* Can't you? Isn't that
how the disciples got by?

DOTTY. Very funny, young lady. You know,
there's a coffee shop up the street where
I could have this thing—free of lip
service.

RAE. *(Under her breath, arranging chairs as
CHARLIE continues to bring them)* Better
them than me.

DOTTY. *(A thought occurs to her)* My *word!*

RAE. *(Worried she'd been heard)* What?

DOTTY. I forgot highlighters and pens.

CHARLIE. *(Up by JEREMY, who is still reading)*
     Have you finished yet?

RAE. *(To DOTTY)* I may have some lying
     around.

JEREMY. Not yet.

CHARLIE. Are you close?

JEREMY. You can clearly see that I'm literally
     almost at the very end of this book.

RAE. Jeremy, would you mind digging around
     for some pens, maybe some
     highlighters?

*(He is torn. It's the age-old depiction of a reader
     full of angst at being asked to abandon
     his story.)*

CHARLIE. I'll look.

RAE. Thank you.

DOTTY. And tables!

CHARLIE. Tables. Got it. *(She exits.)*

PETER. *(Entering with a crate of books in his hands, catching sight of RAE)* Well, look at you, gorgeous.

CUSTOMER. Shhh.

PETER. My apologies. *(He reaches into the crate and produces a hardback tome.)* Is this what you were looking for?

CUSTOMER. Yes. *(Immediately dives into the book)*

PETER. *(Paused for a moment, as if awaiting a "Thank you" upon not receiving one)* You're welcome.

DOTTY. *(As if noticing RAE's clothes for the first time)* Rae Ellen. What are you wearing?

RAE. Clothes, Dot. Clothes.

*(CHARLIE reappears with highlighters and
        pens, distracting DOTTY for the
        moment.)*

CHARLIE. Where do you want these?

DOTTY. On a table or two would be nice.

CHARLIE. Oh. Right *(Exits. DOTTY watches
        her go, shaking her head.)*

PETER. *(Approaching RAE)* Weren't you going
        to head out early this afternoon?

RAE. That was the plan *(A look at DOTTY).*
        Trying to help set things up before our
        weekly Bible study group arrives.

PETER. Isn't that why I'm here? To help step in
        when this place is busy and you need to
        … see to other things?

RAE. Well, yes, but—

PETER. Don't worry. I'll take care of everything.

CUSTOMER. Excuse me. This book smells a
          little. Don't you have another copy?

PETER. *(Being congenial)* I'm sure we don't.
          You know these old books. They tend to
          soak up the, uh, atmosphere of whatever
          place they're stored in.

CUSTOMER. I guess I hadn't considered that.
          Atmosphere, huh? *(Opening the book
          and taking a sniff between the pages)*
          This atmosphere is musty. I want another
          one.

PETER. May I? *(The CUSTOMER hands the
          tome to him. He pauses to take a sniff.)*
          Smells fine to me.

CUSTOMER. Can I at least get a discount?

PETER. *(Getting a bit annoyed now)* It costs
          three dollars.

CUSTOMER. More with tax.

RAE. I'll knock off ten percent for you. How
     does that sound?

CUSTOMER. Fine. *(Retrieving the book from
     PETER's hands, the CUSTOMER sits in
     an armchair. PETER shrugs, then takes
     off down an aisle with the crate of books).*

*(Under the above, CHARLIE has carried a few
     small tables into the space. DOTTY
     hovers, scrutinizing each one).*

DOTTY. That one's dusty.

CHARLIE. I'll be sure to wipe them all down
     *(Moving to grab a rag and cleaning
     solution from behind the bar).*

DOTTY. Thank you. I'm going to use the little
     reader's room and I'll be right back. *(Exits
     toward the restrooms)*

RAE. *(Quickly approaching PETER, who has
     made his way back into the main space
     without the crate)* Can I talk to you for
     just a second?

PETER. Why, what's wrong?

RAE. What? Nothing. Why would something be
    wrong?

PETER. I don't know. In my experience when
    an employer says they need to talk to
    you, it's because you're getting canned.

RAE. Peter, you're one of my oldest friends.
    Why would I fire you?

PETER. Just a reflex, I guess.

RAE. Oh. Well, anyway. I have a favor to ask.

PETER. Okay. Shoot.

RAE. Calvin and I are going to dinner.

PETER. And?

RAE. I would appreciate it if you could keep
    Dotty occupied when Cal and I get back.

PETER. When you get—surely their Bible study won't last that long?

RAE. It won't. But she'll want to oversee putting things away after it's over. She tends to linger.

PETER. Oh. Okay, I'll keep her distracted.

RAE. Thank you. And, Peter?

PETER. Hm?

RAE. When we do get back … Don't let Jeremy go upstairs for a while.

PETER. I could see if he and Charlie wanted to grab dinner or something. How long are you wanting him out of here?

RAE. As long as it takes.

PETER. Sure. *(A thought)* Does Jeremy live up there with you guys? He's here a lot.

RAE. Sometimes it feels like it, Peter.
Sometimes it really does.

*(CALVIN appears from upstairs, dressed for a
night out, and with a certain zip in his
step).*

CALVIN. *(Spotting RAE; gesturing)* My beautiful
wife—

CUSTOMERS. Shh!

CALVIN. *(A bit sarcastically, quieter)* Ah, the
never-ending chorus. *(He descends the
stairs, meeting his wife on the ground
floor. PETER disappears down one of the
aisles of books.)*

RAE. Hi, handsome.

CALVIN. You ready?

RAE. Think so. Let me grab a jacket really
quick. *(They kiss, letting it linger for a bit.)*

JEREMY. *(Not looking up from his book)* Ew.

CALVIN/RAE *(Breaking apart)* Sorry.

RAE. I'll be right back. *(Quick kiss before disappearing upstairs)*

DOTTY. *(Reemerging, with a paperback in her hands. She crosses to CHARLIE and shoves it toward her.)* That was left in the religious section.

CHARLIE. Oh. Thank you? *(She plops it on the checkout counter before stowing the rag and cleaning solution.)*

DOTTY. Calvin.

CALVIN. Dot.

DOTTY. *(Snatching the book back up)* If you can't keep these bare-breasted Jezebels out of the religious section, how can we possibly—are you wearing lipstick?

CALVIN. Rae's, probably.

DOTTY. It makes you look rather silly.

CALVIN. *(Straightening his shoulders)* Well.
Who asked you, anyway?

DOTTY. *(Thrusting the book at him)* Keep the
smut *out* of the devotionals, if you please.

*(CALVIN nods graciously, taking the book
toward the Romance section. Meanwhile,
JEREMY snaps his book shut. CHARLIE
looks at him expectantly.)*

CHARLIE. Did you finish it?

JEREMY. What do you think?

CHARLIE. And?

JEREMY. You're right. Almost identical.

RAE. *(Entering, purse in hand and jacket
draped over her shoulder)* All right, Dotty.
I'm heading out. If you need anything, let
Peter know.

DOTTY. He knows not to close until we're finished, right?

RAE. Of course he does. *(CALVIN reappears, bookless)* Ah, there you are.

CALVIN. Here I am.

CHARLIE. You guys have a good evening. *(She is met with a glare from a nearby CUSTOMER.)*

RAE. Thanks, Charlie. *(They move to exit).*

DOTTY. Calvin. Don't forget your lips. Red isn't your color.

CALVIN. Well. I think I look great. *(Giving DOTTY a once-over; Taking his wife's purse; Privately, to RAE)* Her shoes are gauche. *(Exits through the front door to the street with a flourish)*

DOTTY. Excuse me—

RAE. You guys have a good evening! *(As she exits)* Bye!

(DOTTY makes a "tsk" sound but returns to her study area to finish setting things up. Near the register, CHARLIE and JEREMY are speaking in excited tones.)

CHARLIE. It's almost exactly like the Bailey murder. What do you think that means?

JEREMY. That Colson Graves copied the plot for his novel from a real-life cold case that happened in our town?

CHARLIE. Exactly! Which means he probably lived here when it happened!

JEREMY. We can't know that for sure. How well-known was the murder when it happened?

CHARLIE. Not particularly. I mean Graves wrote it pretty accurately in his book. Elle Bailey wasn't well-known around here. She came from a poor family, just like in

the book. Strangled. Shot. From the
articles I found at the library, police
thought the murderer might be a
boyfriend. But the evidence they
collected was damaged in a fire not long
after the murder took place.

JEREMY. Graves got the fire right, too.

CHARLIE. Sure, there was fluff here and there
to add some texture to the story. But the
basic facts of the case are present in the
novel.

JEREMY. Wow. An award-winning suspense
author may have actually written a story
about a crime that took place in this very
town.

PETER. *(Appearing, as if out of nowhere)*
Whatcha guys talking about?

JEREMY. Nothing.

CHARLIE. *(With quiet excitement)* The new Colson Graves book is based on a murder that took place here.

PETER. *(His face a confused frown)* What?

CHARLIE. Look. *(Pulling her phone out of her pocket, handing it to him)* I have five pieces from the library's digital newspapers. Some have more details than others.

PETER. Ahh …

JEREMY. I've read them. She's right.

PETER. How do you know …

CHARLIE. *(Sliding it in front of him)* Advance reader copy.

PETER. I thought Rae had put this away in her apartment.

JEREMY. Oh. Yeah. I took it.

PETER. Ah.

CHARLIE. I think Graves lives here.

JEREMY. Just because he wrote about Elle
        Bailey's murder doesn't mean he
        lives—or *lived*—here.

PETER. I mean, who's to say whether he does,
        or did? *(He shakes his head)* How? I
        mean. *Wow.*

*(CASSIE enters from an aisle, carrying a few
        books in their arms. They spot DOTTY
        and the chairs downstage. JEREMY,
        CHARLIE, and PETER continue
        pantomiming discussion under the
        following.)*

CASSIE. Is this seat taken?

DOTTY. Why no! You are more than welcome
        to sit.

CASSIE. Why thank you. *(Hugging books to
        their chest)* I just love reading, don't you?

DOTTY. Yes. I'm waiting for my Bible study
        friends.

CASSIE. I go through these moods. Sometimes
        I don't touch a book for months, then, all
        of a sudden, I'm on my tenth in three
        weeks and I just can't wait to lose myself
        in the next one. Funny how life works that
        way. I guess I just get busy sometimes.
        *(DOTTY nods politely but doesn't
        respond.)* What are you reading right
        now?

DOTTY. Well, I—

CASSIE. I've been on a fantasy kick here lately.
        Just look at this— *(Holds a closed book
        up for DOTTY to see)* all these pages.
        The author lived in those pages when
        she wrote this book. And when I start
        reading, I'll get to live in those pages for
        a while too. Like magic.

DOTTY. Hm.

CASSIE. I can hardly stand a sad ending.
        Those are just awful. Don't you think?

DOTTY. You seem familiar to me. Do I know
        you from somewhere?

CASSIE. Oh, probably. I've had lots of jobs.
        First one was a pusher at the Green
        Mart. Then the Taco Shack after high
        school. I worked at the bank for a while.

DOTTY. How long ago was that?

CASSIE. I don't know. Twenty years?

DOTTY. Maybe that's it. *(A pause)* You don't sit
        on the back row at First Methodist, do
        you?

CASSIE. No. I actually have a 10 a.m. class
        scheduled for Sundays.

DOTTY. Oh? What class?

CASSIE. Well, I'm just hosting park classes for
        now, but I'm opening my own yoga studio
        soon.

DOTTY. You what?

*(They continue a quieter discussion under the
        following as PETER, JEREMY, and
        CHARLIE speak louder.)*

CHARLIE. You're not listening. We could be
        marketing this!

PETER. Marketing. *(He looks at JEREMY, who
        shrugs.)*

CHARLIE. The book officially releases on
        Halloween. We could keep the store
        open late, offer candy to the
        trick-or-treaters like normal, but host an
        event inside. We're the sole bookstore in
        the actual town where the *real* murder
        took place.

PETER. Uh …

JEREMY. With a murder mystery game.

CHARLIE. Well—

PETER. Wait, wait. It's the middle of October.
        Not that I'm against hosting something
        that could help the store, but—

(CASSIE gets up, escaping DOTTY, and
        disappears down an aisle of books.)

JEREMY. We could invite Colson Graves to
        come.

CHARLIE. Oh my gosh.

PETER. *What?*

CHARLIE. That's perfect. I wish I'd thought of it.

JEREMY. Well, you didn't, so—

PETER. Guys. Halloween is, what, two weeks
        away? How do you think you're going to
        plan and advertise an event on such

short notice? People probably already
have plans.

CHARLIE. That's right, Jer. What if Graves isn't
available?

JEREMY. I mean, we can still try. *(To PETER)*
Right?

PETER. *(Disappointed)* Right. *(Then:)* Unless
"Colson Graves" is a pen name.

CHARLIE. Oh. Of course.

JEREMY. He could be anybody. Even Dotty.
*(They all look over to the woman in
question, then shake their heads.)*

CHARLIE. Okay. Maybe not Dotty.

JEREMY. And no way is "Colson Graves" a real
name. Which means—

CHARLIE. Even if we could find him, he
probably wouldn't go out of his way to

come to the event. He'd be forced to
reveal his secret identity.

PETER. Hey, listen. You guys can still give
candy out and stuff like that. Keep the
store open. I don't know. Offer ten
percent discounts for people wearing a
costume. *(Neither answer; both are
dismayed at the snag in their plan.)*

CHARLIE. *(An idea coming to her)* Unless.

JEREMY. Unless we still have the event and
market it as we planned. The town
behind the true story behind Colson
Graves's latest thriller—

CHARLIE. Invite him to come—

JEREMY. And if he comes—

CHARLIE. But even if he doesn't—

PETER. Wait.

JEREMY. It's still going to be the biggest thing
        that's ever happened to this place.

CHARLIE. Rae's going to love it. I'll make the
        fliers!

JEREMY. I'll order the—I don't know—I'll order
        something!

CUSTOMERS. *SHHH.*

(LIGHTS OUT.

*During the scene change, the Advance Reader
        Copy (ARC) remains on the counter.)*

SCENE 4

"Coffee, No Coffee"

(LIGHTS UP. The next morning. The store is void of customers. RAE enters from upstairs, dressed in pajamas and a robe. There's a knock from the front door.)

RAE. *(Sweetly)* Coming! *(Nearing the bottom of the steps, she's hit with a quick—but not obvious—spell of nausea.)*

(Knocking continues, more frantic)

RAE. *(Less sweetly)* I said I'm coming!

(She reaches the door, and, upon opening it, PETER races in.)

RAE. Peter—

PETER. Thank you.

RAE. What are you doing here this early? I thought you were Calvin.

PETER. Sorry to disappoint. Uh, how was your
    dinner?

RAE. It was good—

PETER. Great. Great. Glad to hear it.

RAE. Are you all right?

PETER. Sure. Well, maybe.

*(The door opens, and CALVIN enters. He
    carries two to-go cups of coffee.)*

CALVIN. Good morning, my love. Oh. Hello,
    Peter.

PETER. Hi. We may have a problem.

RAE. A problem?

PETER. Yes. Maybe.

CALVIN. *(To RAE)* Your mocha latte.

*(PETER intercepts the offering, taking the cup
from him and taking a sip.)*

PETER. Thank you.

CALVIN / RAE. You're welcome? / Hey!

PETER. *(To RAE)* Pregnant people can't have
caffeine.

RAE. I'm not pregnant yet.

PETER. Still.

CALVIN. Do I need to make another trip up the
street?

RAE. I could just make a pot here. Although
Irene does make the best lattes. *(This is
a hint.)*

CALVIN. *(Matching her tone)* Then that's what
you'll get.

RAE. And a muffin?

CALVIN. Of course.

RAE. *(An idea)* Or maybe, Hilda's? For some
        donut holes and a maple bar or two?

CALVIN. *(His tone no longer playful)* You want
        me to walk half a block that way to
        coffee, then turn around and walk two
        blocks in the opposite direction for
        donuts?

RAE. Only if you don't mind.

CALVIN. *(To PETER)* Translated: I'm getting
        coffee and donuts.

PETER. Later. Right now, we need to talk.
        When are Jeremy and Charlie getting
        here?

RAE. Ten. Why?

PETER. Okay, good. Uh. So there have been
        some developments. Charlie connected
        some dots. She wants to have an event

here and she wants Colson Graves to come.

CALVIN. Charlie figured out that you're Colson Graves?

PETER. No. But she might as well have.

RAE. What event is it that she's wanting to do?

PETER. Basically a launch party. On Halloween. For the book. *(He pauses, hoping for the significance of the announcement to set in. RAE and CALVIN share a puzzled look.)*

CALVIN. Well, she's a fan. I guess it makes sense she'd want to commemorate the day.

RAE. But for one random murder mystery writer? I mean, sure his books are popular, but I don't get a lot of requests for him around here. Unless you count Charlie. And Douglas. But Douglas buys everything, and Charlie usually just reads

what's in stock and puts it back when
she's done. Colson Graves isn't exactly a
household name here. *(Realizing how
that may have sounded; To PETER)*
Sorry. I just mean I'm not likely to host a
launch party for an author people don't
really know about. Oh. Sorry.

PETER. *(Sarcastically)* No, feel free to
continue.

RAE. I mean, of course, you're an
award-winning novelist. It's just that your
books tend to sell well in other places
more than … never mind.

PETER. Well, I'm sorry to hear that my books
don't increase your revenue. Maybe
when Charlie tells everyone that *They
Found Her on Sixth Street* happened *in
this town*, you'll start getting pre-orders
coming out of your nose.

RAE. What?

PETER. *(Typing on his phone)* Elle Bailey
        Murder. *(He hands the phone to her.)*

CALVIN. *(Over his wife's shoulder)* Elle Bailey.
        Oh my gosh. I remember her.

RAE. You remember someone who died in
        (reading) 2002?

CALVIN. I was eight.

RAE. Oh yeah. I forget how old you are
        sometimes.

CALVIN. I'm only three years older than you if
        you recall.

RAE. How should I know? I've never seen a
        birth certificate.

PETER. If you two could take a short break
        from flirting, for just a moment.

RAE / CALVIN. Sorry.

RAE. *(Skimming)* Strangled to death. Then shot
     in the chest. They never found the gun,
     the killer, or what he used to strangle her
     with.

PETER. I didn't realize I'd based the plot on her
     murder. But when Charlie brought it up, I
     remembered hearing about it. Or maybe I
     saw it on the news. I don't know. And I
     don't know why it didn't occur to me
     before. And Charlie thinks Colson Graves
     lives here. Thinks he might come if we
     marketed the release date … and the
     story behind the book.

CALVIN. How would Charlie even know about
     the murder? She's too young to
     remember it. I mean, if Rae doesn't even
     remember it …

RAE. When I interviewed her for her job, she
     told me all about a mayoral scandal from
     the 1980s. *(A shrug)* She's full of true
     crime information.

CALVIN. So. What do you want to do?

PETER. What do you mean?

CALVIN. Charlie isn't wrong. This could mean
          money for the store. Could bring Colson
          Graves a lot of attention. And Peter
          Lochlan, if you wanted.

RAE. Is that what you want?

PETER. *(The thought hadn't occurred to him.)*
          I—don't know.

CALVIN. It might be nice. Making the big reveal
          in your hometown. Probably make you a
          little bit famous. Famous around here
          anyway.

*(The front door opens, and JEREMY and
          CHARLIE enter. CHARLIE holds a brown
          package. They stop when they see RAE,
          PETER, and CALVIN.)*

JEREMY. I'm just saying her face was weird.

CHARLIE. She was dying. What did you want
    her face to be like?

JEREMY. *(Noticing the others)* Oh. Hello. *(To
    CHARLIE)* She didn't have to cross her
    eyes like that is all I'm saying.

RAE. Good morning.

CHARLIE. She won an award for that scene.

JEREMY. That doesn't change the fact that it
    was a weird facial expression.

RAE. Sorry to interrupt. What are you both
    doing here so early? How did you get in?

JEREMY. *(Holding up a key)* Oops.

RAE. When did you get *that? (To CALVIN)*
    When did he get that?

CALVIN. I don't know. He didn't get it from me. I
    thought you couldn't copy those keys.

JEREMY. You can copy any key. It just depends on who you know.

RAE. Give it. *(He does.)* I have a hard enough time keeping you out of our apartment without knowing you're walking around with a key in your pocket.

CHARLIE. Rae, we've got an idea for Halloween.

RAE. I've heard.

(CHARLIE and JEREMY react to RAE's less-than-enthusiastic response).

PETER. I, uh, shared some of your ideas with her.

CHARLIE. Oh. Okay. *(A look at JEREMY)*

JEREMY. We made fliers. *(CHARLIE nudges him.)* Charlie made fliers.

CHARLIE. *(Opening the package and passing some copies around)* I can change

anything you don't like about them.
These are just a mockup.

RAE. You guys have already planned games
for this?

JEREMY. Well, we have a couple of ideas.

CHARLIE. Some will need to be worked out.

CALVIN. You've even got plans for a costume
contest.

CHARLIE. What do you guys think?

RAE. It's late notice to be trying to throw
something like this together.

JEREMY. You make a fair point. However—

CHARLIE. It's on Halloween. People will be in
costumes already.

JEREMY. And the games we're wanting to play
should be free of charge.

CHARLIE. We were already planning on
          handing out candy to the kids.

JEREMY. The costume contest is the only thing
          that should cost any money. Handing out
          the award, I mean.

CHARLIE. We were thinking about giving the
          winner a gift card.

RAE. This is … I mean, you guys showed some
          great initiative. I just. I don't think we
          should do this.

CHARLIE. What?

RAE. Look, I know you're interested in this
          story. But I think—I think you're forgetting
          that this was a real murder that really
          happened in *this* town. And we're going
          to, what, make a party out of it? We're
          going to capitalize off of someone's
          tragedy?

CHARLIE. No, that's not—

JEREMY. I mean, Graves is doing it.

PETER. What?

JEREMY. He's capitalizing off of her murder by
        writing about it.

RAE. I'm sorry, but we're not doing this.

CHARLIE. But—

JEREMY. Wait a minute—

RAE. I'm sorry, but I don't feel right about it.

CHARLIE. *Rae.*

CALVIN. What if we removed the part about the
        book?

PETER. Cal—

CALVIN. We can still do something for
        Halloween. Keep the games. Keep the
        costume contest. Just remove any
        mention of Colson Graves and his book.

(He takes the flier from her hand, stacking it with his, and sets them down on the closest surface—the top of a short rack of shelves.)

RAE. I don't know. *(A look at PETER)* It's still very short notice. How are we going to advertise something like this? *(Seeing how disappointed JEREMY and CHARLIE have become).* Look. I appreciate you guys going out of your way to plan something for the store.

CHARLIE. *(The idea popping into her head)* Bookmarks. What if I made bookmarks for the event, with all the information? And we put the bookmarks in with each purchase leading up to the day of the event?

JEREMY. That combined with a social media event page should bring some people in.

CALVIN. *(With a look to his wife)* I mean, what's the worst that could happen? No one shows up?

RAE. It wouldn't be the first time. *(A beat as
she thinks)* Okay. Okay, let's do it.

CHARLIE. Thank you, Rae!

RAE. Yeah, yeah. *(A glance at her watch)*
We're going to be late opening this place
up if we don't get to work soon. I need to
go get dressed. And Cal?

CALVIN. Coffee?

RAE. Please. And a muffin. I'm so hungry I'm
almost queasy.

CALVIN. On it.

PETER. I'll go with you. *(He adds his flier to
Calvin's pile.)*

*(RAE makes her way toward the stairs. On the
way up, she has to pause as she lets out
a slow and steadying breath—unnoticed
by others on stage—before an idea
occurs to her and she continues quickly*

up the steps. CALVIN and PETER move to the front door. On opening it, they find a CUSTOMER on the other side.)

CUSTOMER. Hi there! Opening up early this morning?

PETER. *(Glancing at his watch)* That wasn't the plan, exactly—

CUSTOMER. *(Ignoring him, entering)* I'll be the first in line to see if you've got anything *new.*

PETER. Uh. Yes. Welcome.

CHARLIE. *(Noticing)* We've got it, guys. Go ahead.

CALVIN. Text us your coffee orders. Peter's treat.

PETER. *(To CALVIN as they exit)* Thanks. That's nice of me.

CUSTOMER. Do you? Have anything new?
Any westerns?

CHARLIE. *(A glance to JEREMY)* Not that I
know of.

CUSTOMER. Hm. I'll glance around. *(They
scurry off down an aisle.)*

*(The front door opens, and DOUGLAS pokes
his head in.)*

DOUGLAS. Good morning! How are you fine
young—*oh goodness!*

*(In a burst, DOTTY rushes through the front
door, practically pushing DOUGLAS out
of her way. Her sights land on CHARLIE.)*

DOTTY. Excuse me, young lady.

JEREMY. Um, Mrs. Jones, I think you just ran
someone—

DOUGLAS. *(Entering)* No worries! I'm in one
piece.

CHARLIE. How can I help you, Mrs. Jones?

DOTTY. I just heard something rather upsetting
     at Office Supply that I would like you to
     clarify for me. *(She glances over at
     DOUGLAS.)* Perhaps in private.

DOUGLAS. Pardon me, Dorothy. But the word
     "private" implies there's gossip. And you
     really shouldn't have used that word if
     you didn't want me gettin' nosey about it.
     What's the scuttlebutt?

DOTTY. This hardly concerns you. Besides, it's
     nothing. Just … boring book talk.

DOUGLAS. Boring book talk? No such thing.

CHARLIE. What is it, Mrs. Jones?

DOTTY. *(A last look to DOUGLAS)* Fine. I was
     just at Office Supply printing my
     Halloween greeting cards when the
     person behind the counter told me

something I rather hope to find is not
true.

CHARLIE. Halloween greeting cards?

JEREMY. I mean, I've heard of Thanksgiving
greeting cards. But you don't usually hear
about people mailing them out for
Halloween.

DOTTY. Excuse me?

DOUGLAS. Now, there's nothing wrong with a
good greeting card. I don't send them
nearly as often as I'd like to.

DOTTY. Thank you, Douglas. If you'll give me
your mailing address, I'll be sure to
include you on my list. *(Digging in her
purse for a pen and pocketbook)*

DOUGLAS. That would be lovely. Thank you,
Dorothy.

DOTTY. Oh certainly! *(JEREMY and CHARLIE
exchange a look, quite certain this is the*

most pleasant they have ever seen this person. Then, back to the matter at hand:) In any case, while the young person with the blue hair was helping me select my card size, he was telling me that you all are going to have an event this Halloween that I find rather upsetting. Tell me, is it true that this new Colson Greaves book is based on Elle Bailey's murder?

CHARLIE. Graves.

DOTTY. What?

CHARLIE. His name is Colson Graves. And we can't say one hundred percent that it's true, but the stories line up. *(To JEREMY)* I wasn't aware we were going around telling people that.

JEREMY. You put it right there on the flier. Luke asked me when I went to pick the order up this morning. What did you want me to say when he asked me about it?

DOUGLAS. I'm afraid I'm a bit lost. What event
    on Halloween? What murder?

DOTTY. Do you remember that girl that they
    found in the laundromat back in '96?

DOUGLAS. No.

CHARLIE. Bank. They found her in a bank. It
    shut down, but there's a grocery store in
    that building now. The one on sixth
    street?

DOUGLAS. Oh, I remember that bank. Pretty
    marble floors. They covered them with
    some cheap laminate or something
    similar. Can you believe that? All that
    beautiful marble.

DOTTY. Am I right in understanding you are
    going to drag that poor girl's death into
    the spotlight so you can tell some ghost
    story on Halloween?

JEREMY. *(To CHARLIE)* Who knew how wildly
    unpopular this idea would be?

CHARLIE. It's a moot point anyway, Mrs.
        Jones. Rae nixed the idea. She voiced
        the same concerns you're having.

DOTTY. I'm glad to hear it.

DOUGLAS. Seems there's nothing much to
        worry over after all. All that fretting over
        nothing, Dorothy.

DOTTY. I guess you're right. Thank you both.
        (She turns to go but stops at the door.)
        Some of us still remember the morning
        we woke up and heard the news about
        that poor girl. She had a sad, hard life. A
        short life. I'm sure I seem ridiculous and
        high-strung to you all. But that girl's
        murder shook this whole town for
        months. We didn't trust anybody after
        that. And we weren't used to that kind of
        fear. Maybe if that writer knew about that,
        he or she wouldn't have written about it.
        (A bit smaller) It's a hard way to live,
        being scared of everybody. I hate to see

us go through something like that again.
(She exits as more CUSTOMERS enter.)

DOUGLAS. Don't mind her. She's always gotta fret about something. Now. I came to spend some money and I don't plan on leaving until I've got a pile of books up over my head. *(He exits down an aisle.)*

(Alone for a moment, CHARLIE and JEREMY give each other a guilty look.)

CHARLIE. I didn't realize people would be so worked up about this.

JEREMY. Not everyone is. Just Dotty Jones.

CUSTOMER. *(To CHARLIE)* Excuse me, young lady. Would you kindly point me to your section on the occult?

CHARLIE. Uh, sure. Are you looking for something specific?

CUSTOMER. The tarot books, please.

CHARLIE. Absolutely. Right this way. *(She leads them down an exit.)*

RAE. *(Entering from upstairs, dressed for the day, and a book in hand)* Jeremy, will you let me know if—well, let's be honest—*when* Dotty comes in today? I've got a book for her.

JEREMY. Oh. She just left. I could run after her—

RAE. No, that's all right. *(Making her way behind the counter, where she attaches a sticky note to the book, leaving the tome on the counter)* She didn't get an opportunity to corner me about something asinine, so I'm sure she'll be back. *(As more CUSTOMERS enter)* Hi, guys. Welcome in.

CUSTOMERS. *(Ad-libbed greeting as they begin perusing the books. As they look, they will unshelve a few items for JEREMY to clean up later.)*

JEREMY. Uh. Yes ma'am.

RAE. Where did those fliers go?

JEREMY. What?

RAE. The manilla envelope with the fliers? We
         probably don't want customers walking
         off with those, at least until we get the
         updated version.

JEREMY. *(Finding it)* Here.

RAE. Oh, good. Let's put those behind the—

*(The front door swings open, and DOTTY
         enters, cutting RAE off.)*

DOTTY. Oh, Rae Ellen! I'd like to speak to you.

RAE. Now, Dot. I have it on good authority that
         you've already been in here today. You
         only get one complaint per visit, per day.
         That's my new rule.

(During the following, one of the CUSTOMERS on stage spots a Halloween flier. CUSTOMERS discuss between themselves. One of them poses with the flier as the other removes their phone from their pocket and snaps a picture. The CUSTOMER holding the flier places it in their bag. The two continue browsing books).

DOTTY. Very charming. I was going to ask you about penning some of us ladies in for a new book club.

RAE. Is this to replace the Bible study, or were you hoping for additional floor time for a different group?

DOT. A different, additional group, if you please.

RAE. Midday or evening?

DOT. Evening.

RAE. Okay. If you'll join me in my office, I'll see what I can do. *(They exit.)*

(JEREMY grabs the manilla envelope, stowing it behind the counter. As he does, the FIRST CUSTOMER of the day reappears. He holds two books in his hands.)

JEREMY. I see you had some luck with the Western section.

CUSTOMER. *(Waving the books)* Yessir, I did. You get any new biographies or wildlife books in?

JEREMY. I can say with a level of certainty that we did not. *(He moves to tidy the few books that have been left out by the previous customers.)*

CUSTOMER. Hm. *(He stops at the shelf holding the remaining fliers. He pauses, picks one flier up, skims it, and has a reaction to the information on the page.*

He folds the flier and pockets it before continuing his perusal of the shelf.)

CHARLIE. *(Reentering)* I just had my palm read.

JEREMY. How'd it go?

CHARLIE. I'm not convinced he/she/they (Gender based on actor) knew what he/she/they was/were) doing. Aren't you supposed to check for lifelines or something like that?

JEREMY. I think so.

CHARLIE. Well apparently all my palm said was that I shouldn't have meatballs this week.

JEREMY. I definitely don't think meatballs are involved.

CHARLIE. That's what I thought. *(A beat)* I knew I shouldn't have forked over $15 to someone looking to buy *Tarot for Beginners.*

JEREMY. Live and learn.

CUSTOMER. *(Approaching the counter)* I believe I'm about finished here.

JEREMY. Sounds good. I'll get you checked out. *(Quickly typing in the POS)* Two used paperback books come to $5.47.

CUSTOMER. *(Digging in wallet before paying)* There ya go.

(RAE and DOTTY emerge from the office.)

DOTTY. Well, you know I would have preferred a Friday. But I appreciate you penciling my little group into your schedule.

RAE. Of course. Oh, and Dot—*(Reaching for the book behind the counter)* this is for you.

DOTTY. Oh, how sweet. Is it good?

RAE. Not sure. I just saw it and thought of you.

DOTTY. *(Making her way to the front door with RAE following)* What a cute picture on the cover. This looks promising. Thank you. Pleasure doing business with you. *(She pauses by the front door to shake RAE's hand.)*

(Just as DOTTY opens the door to exit, CALVIN reappears with a coffee in hand.)

CALVIN. Dotty. Good morning.

DOTTY. Good morning, sir. And goodbye. I'll be seeing you at choir practice. *(She exits; he holds the door for her before entering fully.)*

RAE. You made it back fast. Where are the donuts?

CALVIN. Patience, patience. I decided I'd stop by with your coffee first before I went that

way. Wouldn't want you expiring from
caffeine withdrawal.

RAE. It's a bit late for that, I'm afraid.

CALVIN. Hey, blame Peter. He's the one who
stole your first drink.

RAE. He can have this one too.

CALVIN. What?

RAE. I decided I'm not in the mood for coffee
right now.

CALVIN. Couldn't you re-decide to be? I've
made two trips now.

RAE. I mean, it sounds good. It's just that I
probably should look into what my
caffeine limits are supposed to be.

CALVIN. But it's a mocha. With whip. And
drizzle.

RAE. Yeah.

CALVIN. When in your life have you ever
        turned down anything with espresso and
        chocolate syrup?

RAE. Right now. *(Making sure no one is
        looking, she pulls something out of her
        pants pocket and drops it into his shirt
        pocket.)*

CALVIN. What are you— *(He pulls the object
        out; blinks.)* Are you—are *you? (She
        nods).* Holy shi—. Shoot. Shoot. *(He
        laughs, picking her up and twirling her.)*

RAE / CUSTOMERS. Shhh!

CALVIN. Sorry. You— *(setting his wife down)*
        you stay right here. *(Gently squeezing
        her stomach with one hand.)*

RAE. Quit smooshing my stomach. There's
        nothing to feel right now.

CALVIN. Sorry. You're right. Sorry. *(She gently
        pushes his hand away.)* Okay. One

minute. I'm going to be right back. Right back. Donuts. *(He grabs her, kissing her before he disappears through the door as CASSIE enters. When outside, he lets out a loud laugh that makes CASSIE puts a hand up to her ear closest to CALVIN.)*

RAE. *(To CASSIE)* Sorry.

CASSIE. Oh, no worries. *(To herself as she crosses away)* I didn't need that ear.

JEREMY. *(Approaching RAE)* Everything okay?

RAE. Sure. Cal's just ... in a great mood.

JEREMY. Oh.

CASSIE. That cranky lady isn't coming back, is she?

RAE. I don't think so.

CASSIE. Oh, thank goodness. I'm sorry to be rude, but she sure can pick at ya.

RAE. I know exactly what you mean.

*(DOUGLAS chooses this moment to reenter,
his arms full of books.)*

RAE. Find anything, Douglas?

DOUGLAS. Not a thing. *(He laughs.)*

RAE. I'll get ya checked out.

DOUGLAS. Many thanks. *(A book tumbles from
his pile as they make their way toward
the counter. JEREMY stoops to retrieve
it.)*

JEREMY. Got it.

*(CASSIE has by now reached the shelf with the
remaining flier. She has been reading it.
Upset, she pockets the paper.*

LIGHTS OUT.

*In the scene change, the ARC leaves the
counter with any other books.)*

ACT TWO

"I Saw It at Gale's"

(At rise: dim lighting and the sound of rain, the very next day. It's a dreary October afternoon. An umbrella rack rests by the front door. On a sign by the front door: "YOGA—2:30" A CUSTOMER or two rest in chairs as they read their latest finds. PETER, relaxing on a stool behind the counter, is also enjoying a book. The setting is altogether peaceful.

Then, it isn't. JEREMY enters from upstairs in a huff, before shutting the door behind him—not a slam, but not gently. The noise startles everyone on stage, but CUSTOMERS quickly relax into their chairs.)

PETER. *(As JEREMY reaches the bottom of the stairs)* Everything okay?

JEREMY. Yeah. Just kicked out of the
      apartment again.

PETER. Rae and Calvin's apartment?

JEREMY. Yeah. Something about how it's "my
      day off" and "don't I have any hobbies."

PETER. You could take up hiking. I know a
      local trail guide that's pretty popular
      around here.

JEREMY. Funny.

PETER. I'd offer to give you something to do
      here, but, like you already said.

JEREMY. I know, I know. I'm not supposed to
      be here.

(CHARLIE enters. She wears a raincoat with
      the hood pulled up over her head. She
      pulls the hood down as she crosses
      toward PETER and JEREMY.)

PETER. That didn't take long.

CHARLIE. Nope. They were quick. *(She pulls a brown envelope from inside her coat and glances behind her.)* Oops. looks like I might've tracked water in.

JEREMY. I got it. *(He moves toward a closet to get a mop).*

CHARLIE. Thanks. Isn't it your day off?

(JEREMY makes a point to ignore the question. He finds a mop and quickly gets to work on the small water trail behind CHARLIE.)

PETER. He's bored. How'd they turn out?

CHARLIE. Pretty great, if I may say so. *(She pulls a few stacks of bookmarks out of the envelope, passing one to PETER to examine.)* I thought we'd stock some up here and scatter a few on tables around the store.

PETER. I like it.

(RAE enters from upstairs, a rolled-up yoga mat tucked under one arm.)

CHARLIE. Great! Be right back. *(She collects some bookmarks and starts making her way around the store to distribute them, starting with the tables on stage before slipping off down an aisle.)*

RAE. I almost forgot; we'll need to move some of the shelves around for— *(Catching sight of JEREMY)* What are you doing?

JEREMY. Uh. Cleaning up rainwater?

RAE. Oh. Thanks. Peter, would you mind helping me move some shelves out of the way to make space for Cassie?

PETER. Sure.

(As they move, DOTTY, dressed for rain, enters frantically.)

DOTTY. *Rae Ellen.*

RAE. *(Privately)* One day. Not one day do I get a break from her tyranny—

DOTTY. *(As she reaches them, pulling the book from her purse)* I need to speak with you. Privately.

RAE. I'm a tad busy at the moment, Dot.

DOTTY. This book—*(She waves it in front of RAE's face.)*

RAE. What about it?

DOTTY. I read it last night.

RAE. That fast? I kind of thought I'd have more time to brace myself for this encounter.

DOTTY. I stayed up reading half the night. Half the night, Rae Ellen, before I realized what you'd done.

RAE. Ah.

DOTTY. It's a *dirty story.* This cute little cover
    with the dog and the girl and her
    shopping bags. It's deceptive!

JEREMY. *(Pulling his phone from his pocket)*
    Hey!

RAE. You didn't like it.

JEREMY. I'm not busy. What's up? *(He
    disappears into the office with the mop.)*

DOTTY. Didn't like it? I-- *(Almost in disbelief)* I
    haven't had a story grip me—I mean just
    hook me on the first page and keep me
    reeled in like that. Rae Ellen, I haven't
    read a book that fast in years.

RAE. So you're not mad?

DOTTY. The naughty bits
    notwithstanding—although, I don't
    suppose I *dis*liked them, mind you.

RAE. She is the master of the slow-burn
    romance novel. You know, Dot. I made a

little mistake when I gave you that book. It's actually a sequel.

DOTTY. What?

RAE. Mmhm. The second one in the series. I meant to give you the first book.

DOTTY. Oh. Well. I, um. I suppose I could go take a peek. In the romance section. See if I might find it.

RAE. As it happens *(Going behind the counter),* I have it right here.

DOTTY. How much?

RAE. Consider it a gift. *If* you stop hounding me about the books I sell in the store.

DOTTY. *(A thought)* All right.

RAE. And you're welcome to stay and read for a while. Though we do have a yoga class this afternoon.

DOTTY. *(Alarmed)* Yoga?

RAE. That's not going to bother you, is it?
     (Holding the book closer to her chest)

DOTTY. *(A thought)* No. No, it won't.

RAE. Good. Enjoy *(Giving it to her).* I need to
     finish setting things up. Let me know if
     you need anything.

(Behind the counter, the store phone rings.)

DOTTY. Thank you. *(She finds a seat.)*

RAE. *(Into the phone as she reaches the
     counter)* Rae's Books, how can I help
     you? *(She listens.)* Yes, we'll be open
     late on Halloween. *(Pause)* Uh, as long
     as people are out trick-or-treating, I
     guess. *(More listening)* Oh, yes. Adults
     can participate in the costume contest.
     (Even more listening) Colson Graves?
     I'm sorry. Where did you say you saw the
     flier? Really? I wasn't aware we'd posted
     any at Gale's. *(Looking across to*

JEREMY as he emerges from the office)
Uh-huh. Thank you. We'll see you then.
(She hangs up.)

JEREMY. Hey, uh, Rae?

RAE. Jeremy.

JEREMY. I have a question about something
     that may or may not be my fault.

RAE. Oh?

JEREMY. Yeah, uh. So. My friend at the
     printers'. With the hair.

RAE. Luke.

JEREMY. Yeah, Luke. He, um. Well, you know.
     Works there.

RAE. I think we've established that Luke works
     at Office Supply, yes.

JEREMY. Oh, we have? Okay. Good. That's
     good. *(A thought)* You know what? This

can wait. It's my day off. I'm technically
not even here. I should go.

RAE. No no. *(As PETER is crossing near them)*
Peter.

PETER. What's up?

RAE. Jeremy has something he wants to tell
me. I have a feeling you should hear it.

JEREMY. You know, it could just as likely be
Charlie's fault as mine. *(After a beat,
during which RAE gives him a stern look)*
Okay. Luke may or may not have printed
extra copies of our Colson Graves flier
and he may or may not have told a lot of
people that Graves is going to be at the
store on Halloween.

PETER. What? Tell him to take them down!

RAE. It's too late. People are finding out. I just
got a phone call about it.

JEREMY. Hey, don't be mad at me. Luke did it.

RAE. I'm not mad at anyone.

PETER. You're not?

JEREMY. I don't even really see what the big
      deal is. The murder happened, what,
      twenty years ago?

RAE. Jeremy, I said I'm not mad.

JEREMY. Oh. Good. Well. Before you change
      your mind, I think I'd better go—

RAE. Nope.

JEREMY. No?

RAE. You've got calls to make. Emails to write.

JEREMY. I do?

RAE. People have been promised Colson
      Graves. There's a flier out there with our
      store name on it making promises about
      a bestselling author showing his face in

my store. I'd say you're at least ninety percent to blame for that little mishap, and you'd probably better get to work finding Mr. Colson Graves so you can invite him to our little event.

PETER. I don't think he's going to be available.

RAE. I guess we're just going to have to find out, aren't we?

JEREMY. *(A pause)* Right. Let me go get my laptop and I'll … get right on that. *(He exits out the front door as CASSIE enters.)*

RAE. Jeremy?

PETER. Um. Rae?

RAE. Yes?

PETER. What are you doing? You know Colson Graves can't be here.

RAE. I know. It wouldn't kill him to have to
        sweat about it a little though, would it?

PETER. I … guess not?

RAE. Exactly.

CASSIE. *(Approaching)* Hi, Rae!

RAE. Cassie! Hi. I'm so glad you're here.

CASSIE. Thank you for inviting me! I've never
        led a class inside a bookstore before.

RAE. Well, let's hope this is the first of many
        classes.

CASSIE. Absolutely! *(A small beat)* Hey, can I
        ask you a question?

RAE. Sure.

CASSIE. Um. When I was in here the other
        day, I saw your Halloween flier?

RAE. Oh.

CASSIE. I don't mean to be a pill, and you
        certainly didn't ask my opinion, but I just
        feel like I should say … well, I don't know
        that I would want to ... *(She huffs.)* Sorry.
        I get tongue-tied. Do you think it's true?
        That Colson Graves person wrote about
        the night Elle Bailey died?

RAE. I think it is. But, Cassie, that flier was a
        mistake. I know there are people around
        here who lived through that whole thing,
        and we're *not* making Halloween about,
        well, about that.

CASSIE. I see.

RAE. I'm sorry if it upset you.

CASSIE. It's just… It's not a time I want to have
        to relive if I can help it. I knew Elle. Well, I
        didn't *know* her. She didn't exactly *let*
        people get to know her. *(A beat)* Anyway.
        I don't think it would be good to bring all
        of that up again.

RAE. Of course. I understand.

CASSIE. Thank you. *(She clears her throat.)*
    So. Where do you want me?

RAE. Anywhere you want. If you need more
    space, let me or Peter know.

CASSIE. Will do!

PETER. *(A little wave to CASSIE)* Hello.

(CALVIN enters silently from the main entrance.
    He is carrying an open envelope in one
    hand.)

CASSIE. *(To PETER)* Nice to meet you. *(She*
    shakes his hand.)

RAE. *(CALVIN has reached her elbow and is*
    whispering something in her ear.) The
    real question is, who hasn't?

CASSIE. Huh?

RAE. Nothing. I'll let you get set up and I'll
        check in after a few minutes. Not sure
        what the turnout will be
        today—sometimes these things are hit
        and miss—but you'll at least have me
        following along. Peter, do you have a
        second?

PETER. Yeah.

CASSIE. Okie doke.

*(RAE disappears into her office. PETER
        follows, shutting the door as CASSIE
        finds a spot. She unfurls her mat and
        starts stretching. DOTTY peeks over the
        top of her book at the yoga instructor.
        DOTTY frowns a bit as CASSIE folds into
        a downward dog but soon returns her
        attention to her book.*

(LIGHTS OUT.)

"I Wonder Who It's From"

(At rise: it's nighttime, the same day. RAE, PETER, and CALVIN are arranged in various positions of unease around the space.

CALVIN is on the phone with someone. RAE paces around the seating area. PETER sits, staring into space. The envelope from the previous scene lies on a table in front of him).

CALVIN. *(Into the phone)* Mhm. In the mailbox at my office. *(A pause as he listens)* Yes, just the three of us. We're all still here. *(Pause)* No, no one has touched the envelope except me. *(A glance toward PETER)* We'd rather keep this as private as possible since he wrote it under a pen name-- *(Listening)* Okay. Right. We'll be waiting. *(He hangs up.)*

RAE. Well?

CALVIN. They pretty much confirmed what we were thinking. Two officers—investigators? I don't know. They'll be here for the envelope. They want to get my fingerprints to compare with any on the envelope or the letter. They'll want to talk to both of you. Especially Peter.

PETER. I'm sure I don't know anything that will—

CALVIN. They practically named you in the letter, Peter.

PETER. No, they didn't.

RAE. They referred to "the young Mr. Graves," whoever it is. They assume Colson Graves is here with us. Or at least that we know who he is.

PETER. *(Leaning toward the envelope)* Let's read it again to make sure—

RAE / CALVIN. Don't!

CALVIN. Let me. *(Grabbing the envelope)* My
    fingerprints are already on it, remember?

PETER. Can you even get prints off of paper?
    Isn't it too—porous—or something?

RAE. I don't know.

CALVIN. Yes. At least I think you can. *(He
    gently puts the envelope on the table and
    opens the letter. Reading:)* Dear Mr.
    March, Is it true you're having a party in
    my honor this Halloween? I wonder that I
    wasn't invited. Though, I had no way of
    knowing, after all these years, that
    someone would come to care enough
    about that dead girl to write about her
    story. I wish the young Mr. Graves would
    have considered my feelings on the
    subject first. I find it rude. Borderline
    disrespectful. After all, Mr. March, without
    me, there is no story. And if I'd wanted
    someone to write about that dead girl, I
    wouldn't have killed her. Unfortunately,
    you and your little wife—

RAE. *(Rolling her eyes)* Please—

CALVIN. *(Continuing)* "have been dragged into
        this rather dreary situation. I do wish you
        had left my story out of your little
        Halloween party's advertisements. You
        see, I don't wish to have my story told by
        anyone except me.

PETER. I didn't *know* I was telling someone
        else's story when I wrote the book!

CALVIN. "It would behoove the staff of Rae's
        Books to remove any mention of my story
        from the evening's docket. I would hate
        to have any conflict between us. Finally,
        Mr. March, I ask that you cancel any
        invitations you may have offered to the
        young Mr. Graves. I do not want to see
        his face at your store. The conflict I
        mentioned would be most effectively
        avoided this way. I look forward to seeing
        you on Halloween night. I trust you'll be
        keeping an eye out for me as well." *(He*

folds the letter, returns it to the envelope, and leaves them both on the table.)

RAE. *(Rolling her eyes)* Men.

PETER. How do you know it's a man?

RAE. It's *my* store. Yet they're writing to my husband at work? It's a man.

CALVIN. I think the fact it came to me at work tells us a lot about the person.

RAE. The man.

CALVIN. Fine. Yes. For example, he knows where I work.

PETER. I could write a book about this.

RAE. Maybe make sure they've caught the guy the next time you base one of your books on a true story.

PETER. Right.

RAE. Ugh. Jeremy and his big mouth.

CALVIN. We've got to find out how many fliers are out there and take them down.

RAE. I don't know that we can. I've already gotten calls from people asking about it. I had ten calls today from people asking to preorder the book.

PETER. Ten?

RAE. That's a lot for a town this size. More than I've ever gotten before, anyway. This afternoon three people told me they think we're inviting trouble by dragging all of this out into the light again. And everyone wanted to know if the real Colson Graves would really be here on the night of the launch.

CALVIN. In other words, people know about the event. And trying to cancel it at this point …

PETER. It might draw more attention than
    ignoring the commotion altogether.

RAE. *(A groan)* I don't know. I didn't pay
    attention when they covered "How Not to
    Piss off a Murderer" in business class.

CALVIN. What do you want us to do?

RAE. I guess … wait and see what the police
    have to say. And tomorrow, I, well, I
    guess we try to take down as many
    posters as we can. Limit the damage?

CALVIN. Okay.

PETER. I'm sure it'll be fine. Besides, who's
    spending their Halloween at a bookstore?

CALVIN. Right. And I'm sure we can ask the
    police to drive past the store during the
    event. Just a few times, just enough to
    keep an eye on things.

RAE. Okay. *(Then, with more confidence)* Yeah.
    Okay.

PETER. Okay.

RAE. And for now we just … wait.

CALVIN. Yes.

PETER. Do we tell Jeremy and Charlie about
      the letter?

RAE. No. No, I don't want them worrying. As far
      as they know, it's business as usual.
      (She sighs.)

CALVIN. Look at us. Practically parents already.

(Someone knocks on the front door.)

RAE. I guess that's the police?

CALVIN. Probably.

RAE. *(Letting out a breath)* Okay. Let's do this.
      *(She rises, crossing to the front door. She
      reaches for the handle as the LIGHTS
      GO OUT.)*

SCENE 3

"Mr. Graves"

(LIGHTS UP on a full and busy bookstore. CUSTOMERS—including DOTTY—in various costumes stand in an awkward line near the checkout counter. CASSIE is dressed as the Fairy Godmother.

CHARLIE, behind the counter, checks out a customer who is either in street clothes or is otherwise not participating in the contest.

JEREMY, RAE, and PETER sit downstage with notebooks and pens in their laps. RAE looks embarrassed, PETER looks confused, and JEREMY looks altogether frustrated. In front of them, a CUSTOMER strikes a pose in their Halloween costume. CALVIN stands nearby.

Catwalk-esque music plays softly in the background. Minor decoration throughout.

*Near the checkout counter, a small pile of
copies of* They Found Her on Sixth Street
*sits next to a sign announcing the book's
availability.*

*DOUGLAS is mid-catwalk, presenting his
Halloween costume to the judges.)*

JEREMY. Next!

*(RAE and PETER offer polite applause as
DOUGLAS makes his way to the end of
the line and DOTTY approaches).*

JEREMY. Don't forget you're being judged for
being in character too! *(DOTTY does not
do this to his liking, so he jots something
in his notebook.)* Next!

*(More of the same. The next customer
approaches, striking a pose as they
reach the judges on the couch.)*

JEREMY. *(To RAE)* It's like these people don't *want* to win gift cards to local small businesses.

(The CUSTOMER before him tries even harder to make a good impression).

JEREMY. NEXT!

(This CUSTOMER finishes their turn, and CASSIE approaches.)

RAE. Jeremy, don't you think you're being a bit, well—

JEREMY. The prize is equivalent to cash money, Rae. If I wanted crappy performances from people in crappy costumes I would have asked Charlie and her friends to go as witches or something.

CHARLIE. I heard that.

JEREMY. You were supposed to. NEXT.

DOUGLAS. Uh. I think that was the last one of us.

(Nods and other appropriate reactions from all participating.)

JEREMY. Ah. Good. *(He stands.)* Thank you for participating. There will be a brief recess while the judges make a decision. *(He heads toward the office.)*

(Looking sheepish, RAE and PETER follow.)

JEREMY. *(Stopping just outside the office. To CHARLIE)* You're supposed to kill the catwalk music now.

CHARLIE. Oops. *(She mutes the music as the "judges" disappear into the office.)*

(In no time, the CUSTOMERS are milling about and talking among themselves.)

A CUSTOMER. I really liked your costume.

SWAMP MONSTER CUSTOMER. Thanks! I
    won a contest last year; thought I'd try
    my luck again.

(Somewhere else on stage:)

DOTTY. *(To DOUGLAS)* And what are you?

DOUGLAS. I'm a detective. *(He almost looks
    the part in a long coat and a faded red
    scarf, although perhaps a bit odd in a
    bowler hat.)*

DOTTY. You don't look like a detective.

DOUGLAS. Well, I got my deerstalker confused
    for my bowler.

DOTTY. Your what?

DOUGLAS. My hat. *(Tipping it forward with a
    smile.)*

DOTTY. Oh.

DOUGLAS. Mhmm.

DOTTY. Well, aren't you going to ask me what I
    am?

DOUGLAS. Um. What are you?

DOTTY. *(Gesturing to an open, blank journal
    that she has rigged up like a low-hanging
    necklace)* I'm an open book!

*(DOUGLAS laughs heartily. Then, in another
    area of the stage:)*

THIRD CUSTOMER. Do you think they really
    got Colson Graves?

FOURTH CUSTOMER. I don't know.

FIFTH CUSTOMER. I hope he shows. I want to
    get my book signed.

THIRD / FOURTH. Me too.

*(The office door swings open—and out come
    JEREMY, RAE, and PETER.)*

CALVIN. Contestants, it seems as though the
	judges have their results. And it didn't
	take very long.

JEREMY. Some things are obvious.

RAE. *(A bit quietly)* Jeremy? Let's cool it on the
	prima-donna judge thing, okay?

JEREMY. Oh. Right. *(He clears his throat)* Here
	are your winners. In third place, we have
	our Open Book. *(A reaction from DOTTY)*
	Decent move, showing up as a book to a
	costume contest in a bookstore. You win
	a $5 gift card to Gale's Coffee Shop and
	a goodie bag full of Halloween candy.

Next, we have the Fairy Godmother in second
	place. *(A reaction from CASSIE)* You win
	one free class at Cassie's Yoga Studio
	*(RAE and PETER make embarrassed
	faces)* and … a goodie bag of candy.

CASSIE. But I own Cassie's Yoga Studio. *(RAE
	hides her face in her hands)*

JEREMY. Oh.

RAE. We'll make that a $10 gift card to a
    business of your choosing, then, Cass.
    (A reaction from CASSIE)

JEREMY. Finally. In first place. Drumroll,
    please. *(A brief pause as some
    customers, and CHARLIE, comply)* Your
    first-place winner: the Swamp Monster!

*(Polite clapping from some; a bit of
    disappointment from others)*

SWAMP MONSTER CUSTOMER. I thought
    they hated me.

JEREMY. Our first-place winner receives a $15
    gift card to Rae's Books … and,
    apparently, a free class pass to Cassie's
    Yoga Studio. Oh. And a bag of candy.

CHARLIE. *(Making her way toward Center)*
    Thank you, Jeremy. How about a nice
    round of applause for our judges? *(A
    pause as everyone claps, though with*

varied levels of enthusiasm) Now, for our next event. In honor of the holiday, we've taken two horror novels out of their genre section and have stored them in separate areas of the store. The two customers who find these special books and bring them to me will receive a free book of their choosing!

SOME CUSTOMERS. I mean, a used book here is only like two dollars. / I feel like I would've gone for something different. / (Other ad-libbed responses)

CHARLIE. Oh, I forgot. Any *new* book of your choosing. But before you go grabbing just any old horror novel, I should warn you that the winning books have special vouchers in them.

CUSTOMERS. *(Ad-libbed responses as they disperse)* Oh, in that case / Hey, I would've been fine with an old copy.

CHARLIE. Good luck! *(To her coworkers)* I think it's going well. I mean, people showed up. Right?

JEREMY. Yeah, I guess. *(He crosses downstage, finding a chair to sink into.)*

CHARLIE. *(To RAE)* What's got him?

RAE. I don't know.

PETER. What's up, Jeremy?

JEREMY. I'm just kind of ready to be done with all of it.

CHARLIE. Why? I thought you were looking forward to it.

JEREMY. I was. I just—I mean—I really thought Graves would be here.

RAE. *(A look at PETER)* I'm sorry, Jeremy. We knew it was a long shot.

JEREMY. I know. I just. I don't know. I guess I
        was just convinced somehow that he'd
        make it.

PETER. You were? *(JEREMY shrugs.)* I'm, uh,
        sorry to hear that.

JEREMY. It's fine. Everything was so rushed.
        He probably hasn't even seen my
        messages. It is kind of silly, expecting a
        big author like that to show up here.

(A CUSTOMER enters, carrying a book.)

CUSTOMER. Excuse me, I think I found one of
        the vouchers.

CHARLIE. That fast? Um, sure. Can I see it?
        *(The CUSTOMER hands her the book.
        She opens it and pulls out a printed
        card.)* Yup! There's the voucher.
        Congrats! You're welcome to select your
        free book tonight, or—

CUSTOMER. I know what I want: *They Found Her on Sixth Street.* And I was hoping to get it signed. He will be here, won't he?

CHARLIE. Um.

RAE. Colson Graves wasn't able to commit to tonight's event.

CUSTOMER. But your posters said—

RAE. I'm sorry.

CUSTOMER. You know, that's kind of false advertising.

(Other customers start filing back in. DOTTY's holding the other winning book.)

CALVIN. *(Quietly)* Uh oh.

RAE. You're not wrong. And I do want to offer my apologies to anyone who was hoping to meet him tonight. It just … wasn't possible.

ANOTHER CUSTOMER. Wait, Colson Graves isn't coming?

THIRD CUSTOMER. *(To a friend)* I wanted to ask him about the murder.

FOURTH CUSTOMER. Have any of you actually gotten to speak with him? What's he like?

JEREMY. No, we—

RAE. *(Thinking on her feet)* I have. I've spoken with him, uh, on the phone. And he wanted to apologize that he wasn't able to make it. *(More to JEREMY and CHARLIE than anyone else)* He wanted to be here. He did.

DOTTY. Well, I for one am thankful. It's dismal stuff, talking about murderers and being murdered. *(Approaching CHARLIE)* I'll take my prize now, thank you. Rae knows which book I want.

RAE. Right. Um. Thank you, everyone, for
    coming. That sort of concludes our
    planned events for tonight. Feel free to
    stick around and browse for a while.

*(Some ad-libbing as CUSTOMERS begin
    meandering away from the scene. Some
    head toward the front door. Others
    disappear down aisles. Finally, only the
    staff of the bookstore, and DOTTY,
    remain.)*

DOTTY. *(As RAE reaches behind the counter to
    produce a book and gives it to DOTTY)*
    I'm glad I came. And *thank* you for the
    costume prize.

RAE. You're welcome! Glad you could make it.

DOTTY. I had my doubts about the whole thing,
    but I'm glad I didn't leave this story
    *unwritten. (She gestures to the book
    hanging from her neck.)*

RAE. Ah. Good one.

DOTTY. Thank you. I'll be seeing you! *(She heads toward the front door.)*

RAE. Bye, Dot. *(With a sigh, looking at her watch)* You guys can go. Calvin and I can lock up.

CHARLIE. Are you sure you don't want us to help?

RAE. You guys did a great job setting everything up. We'll handle teardown.

CHARLIE. *(Grabbing a bag from behind the counter)* Thanks.

RAE. You're welcome.

CHARLIE. *(To PETER, and to JEREMY, who is still brooding)* You guys coming?

JEREMY. Yeah.

PETER. I'll hang around for a while.

CHARLIE. Oh. Rae.

RAE. Hm?

CHARLIE. Was that true? You've spoken to Colson Graves on the phone?

RAE. Uh, yeah.

JEREMY. Was he, you know, upset that he couldn't make it?

RAE. Yeah. Yes, he was.

JEREMY. *(Nods)* Okay. Goodnight.

(Ad-libbed goodbyes from all.)

CALVIN. *(Settling into a chair)* Please tell me we've successfully avoided any crises.

RAE. *(Joining him)* I hope so.

PETER. What do we do now? Wait for more death threats to show up in the mail?

CALVIN. I guess we just wait. Period.

RAE. We made it through without any major
    issues. Let's just be thankful for that.

(CASSIE appears from one of the aisles,
    holding an armful of books.)

CASSIE. Can I get someone to check me out?

PETER. *(Crossing to the counter)* Of course.

CASSIE. Thanks.

(They start the process of checking out. PETER
    comes to a pause when he gets to the
    last book in the stack: They Found Her
    on Sixth Street.*)*

PETER. Hoping to see what all the fuss is
    about?

CASSIE. Elle and I were coworkers, actually. At
    the bank.

PETER. Oh. Did you know her well? I mean …
    were you friends?

CASSIE. She kept to herself, mostly. Or at least
      she tried to. She was so pretty, the
      good-looking guys always walked up to
      her window. Never did meet a girl who
      rocked red lipstick like Elle. Made the rest
      of us kind of jealous. *(Gathering her
      things)* Thanks.

PETER. Yeah. I mean, you're welcome.

CASSIE. Could I, uh, use your restroom for a
      sec? Didn't want to use the restroom
      before the contest and risk wrinkling my
      skirts.

RAE. Oh, of course. Off that way. *(Pointing)*

CASSIE. Thanks. I'll be right back for my
      goodies. *(She exits. PETER watches,
      contemplating her words.)*

CALVIN. Did anyone happen to notice how
      many customers are still floating around
      in this building?

RAE. No.

PETER. We're not very good at this *looking out for our potential killer* thing.

CALVIN. I'll do a walk-through.

RAE. Be careful.

(CALVIN exits down an aisle. RAE watches PETER for a moment.)

RAE. You doing okay?

PETER. I guess. You?

RAE. *(She shrugs.)* Having the police drive by every few minutes helped.

(CALVIN reappears, DOUGLAS on his heels.)

CALVIN. One straggler.

DOUGLAS. *(His arms full of books)* You all have been holding out on me. I come

here at least once a week asking for
something new.

RAE. I went to an estate sale yesterday.

DOUGLAS. Ah. Gently loved tomes from a life
cut too short. *(He dumps the books on
the counter.)*

PETER. Poetic. Ten books? *(Typing into the
POS)* $21.90.

DOUGLAS. Can't turn down a good deal. *(He
pulls a bill and some change from his
pocket and slides it toward PETER.)*

PETER. Who could?

DOUGLAS. Thanks, you all. *(CALVIN meets
him at the door, opening it wide for him.)*
Thank you, good sir.

RAE. Thanks, Douglas!

*(CALVIN locks the door behind him and flips
the OPEN sign to read CLOSED.)*

CALVIN. That's all she wrote.

RAE. Thank God. *(She flops over on the couch.)* Forget cleaning. We'll deal with it tomorrow.

PETER. Sounds like music to my ears.

(A sharp knock comes from the front door. RAE sits quickly. They freeze).

DOUGLAS's VOICE. Hey you all. I think I forgot my keys.

(A collective sigh of relief. CALVIN unlocks the door.)

DOUGLAS. *(Stepping inside)* My apologies, good friends. I tend to lose things.

RAE. Nothing that hasn't happened before, Doug. We'll help you look for them.

CALVIN. We'll look, Rae. You go put your feet up.

RAE. *(Considering, before she rises and begins crossing toward the stairs)* Well. I won't make you tell me twice. I'll be waiting. Goodnight Peter. Douglas. *(She exits.)*

PETER. Any idea where you could have left them?

DOUGLAS. *(With a chuckle)* I'm afraid I've been down most, if not all, of these aisles tonight.

PETER. No worries. I guess we'll all just pick an aisle and go from there.

CALVIN. Sure.

(They part ways, separating down different aisles.

A moment passes. RAE pokes her head out of the apartment door and glances around the room. She has her phone to her ear.)

RAE. Are you sure it can't wait? *(Her annoyed reaction tells us the answer was "no." She crosses downstairs and to the front door. She opens it.)* Dotty, we've talked about this.

DOTTY. I know we have. But something has occurred to me. Rae Ellen, it's very important.

RAE. So you keep saying.

DOTTY. I'd like to speak to you privately.

RAE. It doesn't get much more private than this.

DOTTY. I *mean* I'd like to visit with you upstairs.

RAE. All right, Dot. Come on up.

(They head toward the apartment exit.)

DOTTY. Whose car is that outside?

RAE. *(A joke)* Don't tell me that's what you drove back here to ask me about.

(They exit. A beat, then DOUGLAS reappears.

This is important: DOUGLAS is chipper and friendly almost until the very end. Find the appropriate levels, but the actor should resist the temptation to play up the entire scene.

Upon finding an empty room:)

DOUGLAS. Hello? Peter?

PETER. *(Offstage)* Yeah?

DOUGLAS. We found my keys.

PETER. *(Reentering)* Oh, good. Where's Cal?

DOUGLAS. Oh, he already went upstairs. He said you could lock up.

PETER. Sure.

DOUGLAS. Funny, the way life brings things back around.

PETER. Sorry?

DOUGLAS. I wasn't sure it was you at first. You were a little thing back then. And look how tall you've gotten.

PETER. I don't—

DOUGLAS. We used to be neighbors. Your mother worked late then. My wife and I, we babysat. You used to sleep on our couch all the time. We watched old westerns and ate popcorn. Remember?

PETER. I'm sorry, I can't say I do.

DOUGLAS. *(A bit disappointed)* Ah, no worries.

PETER. Do you still live next door to my mom?

DOUGLAS. No. Lost the house in the divorce. You know how it goes.

PETER. Oh. I'm sorry.

DOUGLAS. Don't be. Turns out I'm much happier divorced than I was married.

PETER. O-okay. That's good?

DOUGLAS. Have you ever been married?

PETER. No sir. *(He heading toward the front door, gesturing for DOUGLAS to follow.)*

DOUGLAS. Best if you avoid it altogether. We make decisions we think will protect us. Like getting married. Or taking a job we don't want. And then in a few years, we find ourselves locked into a life we hate. But what can we do? How do we get out of it and into something that makes us happy? Do you know?

PETER. *(Realization dawning)* Where's Calvin?

DOUGLAS. And then suddenly someone comes along, and they make us think the world might be bigger than our stupid little lives. *(He produces a gun from an inside coat pocket.)* Better than our stupid little low-paying jobs that suck up so much of our time.

PETER. *(Calling out)* Calvin—

DOUGLAS. Our lives, Peter! Do you know how lucky you are to have a career that you enjoy? You don't have to wait for someone to come along and—and fill that void in you. You like your life. But some of us don't get that pleasure. *(A chuckle)* Most of us have to sacrifice ourselves. Put food on the table. Pay the mortgage. You know I've never even left this country? Do you know how lucky people are who get to travel? I didn't get to do that. I had to provide for my family. Every damn day. *(Conspiratorially)* With a family that takes so much, and a job that gives so little, surely you could imagine my joy when I met her.

PETER. Elle?

DOUGLAS. Beauty and wonder and life itself. *(Producing the Advance Reader Copy from another coat pocket)* She was the closest thing to perfection that I'll find in this world.

PETER. Until you killed her, you mean.

DOUGLAS. *(Setting the ARC on a nearby table)* That's the thing about women, Peter. They draw you in with their wide-eyed innocence and sweet, lost voices. *(Pointing the gun at him)* Stay put, now. I'm trying to tell you my version of the story, Mr. Graves. *(A beat)* Oh, but where was I?

(Unseen by the two men, the upstairs door opens. We see RAE and DOTTY for an instant as they see DOUGLAS holding a weapon before DOTTY quickly—and silently—pulls the door almost entirely shut).

PETER. Women?

DOUGLAS. *(Relaxing his aim)* Ah, thank you. You always were polite. Yes. I'm sure you've experienced it by now. They throw themselves at you, begging to be led. To be paid for. Until they're done with you. You have to be done with them first. That's the only way you make it. That's why a single man is a lucky man.

PETER. Uh. Right.

DOUGLAS. Well, now you've got me right where you wanted me, Peter. Though if it's money you want, I'm afraid I can't afford to pay you to be quiet.

PETER. So you're gonna kill me?

DOUGLAS. You know what I did. And I know who you are. Can you think of a more appropriate way of resolving the issue?

PETER. Um. You turn yourself in and I don't get shot?

DOUGLAS. See, that's almost the opposite of what I want to do. *(He raises the gun once more, taking steps toward PETER.)*

PETER. *(Stalling for time; a gesture to the ARC)* Did you like the book?

DOUGLAS. I'll be honest with you. I haven't read it.

(Like a heroine in an old western, DOTTY appears from above; she aims her own gun in DOUGLAS's direction. RAE stands behind her.)

DOTTY. Douglas Wayne, you put that gun down.

DOUGLAS. Dorothy! What an unfortunate surprise. And Rae. I'll be with you both in a moment. You'd better be careful with that, Dorothy. Wouldn't want you hurting yourself.

CASSIE. *(Reentering from the aisle)* Sorry I took so long. This thing is so tricky to get out of and back intooo—my gosh! *(DOUGLAS focuses the gun on her.)*

DOUGLAS. Goodness, Peter. Look at all these people who know our secret now. Do you see now how much pain your book is going to cause? People are going to get hurt because of you.

RAE. Where's Calvin?

DOUGLAS. *(Ever chipper.)* He hasn't left us yet, don't worry. I didn't hit him that hard. I think.

PETER. Oh god. Douglas, I didn't know, okay? I didn't know I was writing about you when I wrote the book or I wouldn't have started. I didn't even know you were the killer until about five minutes ago.

DOUGLAS. Little white lies won't get you anywhere with me. Don't you remember where you were the night Elle Bailey died?

PETER. No, I don't. I don't. I was a kid, Douglas. I was just a kid. I never even heard that name until Charlie— *(He trails off.)* Your scarf.

DOUGLAS. What about it?

PETER. No, I do. I remember. I was sick that night. I could see the front door from where I would lie down on the couch. When I first fell asleep, there was only your coat on the rack. I woke up in the middle of the night, and that red scarf was there, hanging from the same peg as your coat. You're wearing it now. *(Realizing)* It was hers. You used it to kill her, didn't you? And you kept it. God, you wore it in public tonight like a trophy or something. That's really sick.

DOUGLAS. It *isn't* a trophy. It's all I have left of her. It's how I keep her with me.

PETER. No. You took her life from her, and then you took something that belonged to her.

DOUGLAS. I don't suppose you could understand it. *(Short pause)* But, hey, if you're right, I'll take something of yours, too. Your hat, maybe. *(He aims at PETER with finality.)*

RAE. Dotty—

DOTTY. Shh.

DOUGLAS. I wonder who'll write tonight's story? We know it won't be Colson Graves.

(DOTTY and DOUGLAS fire their weapons at once, and LIGHTS GO OUT.

SCENE 4
"I Miss Everything"

(At rise: a tired-looking group sits on available chairs downstage, made up of DOTTY, CASSIE, PETER, RAE, and CALVIN. No one—except CALVIN, who has a bandage on his forehead—appears to be injured. All wear their clothes from the previous scene. Police tape stretches across the front door. Off, flashing red and blue lights can be seen.)

RAE. I need a vacation.

CALVIN. Same.

DOTTY. My sister has the most darling little cabin. Out by a lake. I forget which one. I've never actually been there. You can probably use it.

CASSIE. Oh, how nice!

RAE. Thanks, Dot.

CHARLIE. *(Entering, Jeremy on her heels)* What happened here? What's with all the police outside?

RAE. Douglas tried to kill everyone. Dotty shot him. Now he's in the hospital but hopefully jail after. I think that sums it up, right?

JEREMY / CHARLIE. What?!

PETER. Sure.

DOTTY. Got him right in the shoulder. No casualties. And they make it look so difficult to manage on television.

JEREMY. Everything happens when we're not here.

CHARLIE. So Douglas—

RAE. Murdered Elle Bailey.

CHARLIE. Oh my gosh.

JEREMY. And Dotty was here because?

DOTTY. It had been bugging me. That day that I came over to ask about this event, and he acted like he knew nothing about it. I didn't think anything of it at first. But later I remembered, he talked about the case all the time when the murder first happened. It just didn't sit right with me that he seemed so clueless.

RAE. She came back last night to share her concerns with me, and …

PETER. She was right.

CHARLIE. Let me see if I understand. You sent us home early. Douglas got mad and tried to kill everyone. And Dotty saved the day. *(To CASSIE)* And you?

CASSIE. Inopportune time to pee.

(Ad-libbed agreement from those sitting.)

JEREMY. I knew I shouldn't have gone home early.

CHARLIE. Is there anything you want us to do?

RAE. I don't know. I was thinking of closing the store for the day. This has just all been a lot, and I don't know that I'm ready to be asked to tell the story to every customer that walks in here.

CALVIN. Just wait until you get asked by a news reporter. *(RAE groans.)*

CHARLIE. Well, hey, do you guys want coffee or breakfast or anything? I'm guessing you didn't sleep last night.

RAE. That would be great. I'd love a dirty chai. *(She catches a look from CALVIN.)* Uh. Just a chai.

CASSIE. That's my favorite!

RAE. Aww, me too!

CHARLIE. Anyone else?

DOTTY. Mmm. How about something hot and chocolatey?

CHARLIE. Like a mocha?

DOTTY. Like hot chocolate.

CHARLIE. Okay. Anyone else?

PETER. I'm good.

CASSIE. None for me.

CALVIN. I mean, I could go for a dirty chai.

RAE. Hey, if I can't have caffeine, neither can you.

CALVIN. Nope. Those aren't the rules.

JEREMY. Wait. Why can't you have caffeine?

RAE. Uh.

DOTTY. Rae Ellen, are you pregnant?

RAE. Um. Yes?

(A small flurry of congratulations.)

RAE. We're, uh, not really telling anyone yet, so.

DOTTY. Don't worry. Your secret is safe with us. And the ladies of the party planning committee at my church. We'll make sure your shower is ready whenever you are.

RAE. *(Unconvinced)* Thanks.

JEREMY. Attempted murder and a baby? I'm never leaving work early again. *(He exits through the front door.)*

RAE. We've got to find him a hobby.

CALVIN. Yes, please. A partner. Anything.

DOTTY. Good luck. *(She rises.)* Cancel my cocoa, girl. I figure I need to go home and get cleaned up.

CASSIE. Do you want someone to drive you? You haven't slept.

DOTTY. Aren't you sweet? You know, I think I'll take you up on that offer. Maybe we can drive past your new studio on our way. You can tell me all your plans for it. *(She grabs her purse.)* I'll be around, Rae Ellen.

CASSIE. See y'all! Glad we didn't die last night.

RAE. Bye! *(A beat after the other women exit)* Is it the leftover adrenaline talking, or do I want to name my firstborn after Dotty Jones?

CALVIN / PETER. It's the adrenaline.

CHARLIE. *(Now standing by the front door)* I better go if I want to catch up to Jeremy. But, um, I just wanted you to know ... I'm glad you're all okay.

RAE. Thank you, Charlie. *(Calvin nods.)*

PETER. Wait. *(Rising, crossing to grab something from behind the counter and then approaching CHARLIE)* I was going to give this to you later, but I don't know. Now seems like a good time.

CHARLIE. A copy of *They Found Her on Sixth Street*. Thank you?

PETER. Well, I know you're a Colson Graves fan, so ...

CHARLIE. Right. I kind of had just already bought one yesterday.

PETER. Ah. Well, this one's different. Check the inside cover.

(CHARLIE does as she's told. Her eyes grow wide.)

CHARLIE. Holy-- *(Turning sharply)* I have so many questions. First, coffee. Wait til Jeremy finds out what else he's missed.

PETER. I have a copy for him, too. If you want to wait so he can be surprised.

CHARLIE. I'll consider it. *(Still wonderstruck)* Thank you for telling me.

PETER. You're welcome.

(Charlie gently slides the book into her bag before exiting.)

RAE. What about Colson if it's a boy?

CALVIN. I thought you said you wanted to name him after me.

RAE. Oh.

(LIGHTS OUT.)

Properties List

General Items

- Books (lots and lots; it's best if they look like they are in newer or gently used condition)
- Pens
- Notebooks
- Cash Register
- Point-Of-Sale System
- Sandwich Board
- Money
- Credit Cards
- Black Music Binders and Paper (about 6)
- Music Stands (about 6)
- To-Go Coffee Cups and Lids
- Pregnancy Test
- Umbrella Rack and Umbrellas
- Shopping Sacks
- Yoga Mats (about 2)
- Mop
- Halloween Candy
- Guns (2; with blank bullets)
- Gun Case (Dotty)
- A Purse (Dotty)
- A Bag (Charlie)

- Car Keys (Jeremy)

Printed Props
- Covers for *They Found Her on Sixth Street*
- Covers for Jeremy's Trail Guide
- Halloween Event Fliers
- Halloween Event Bookmarks
- "Now Available" poster for *They Found Her on Sixth Street*

Costume and Makeup Notes By Character

RAE. Simple makeup. Not dressy by nature, most costumes will consist of jeans and sneakers. For events, though, she likes to step it up.

CHARLIE. Spunky and curious by nature, this should be reflected in costumes and makeup. Whether the costume is built around combat boots and a pop of lip color, or something simple and relaxed with natural makeup, Charlie isn't influenced by the styles of others unless Charlie wants to be.

JEREMY. Not very concerned with his looks. Not sloppy; just uninterested in trivial things like matching socks. Dresses up when the situation calls for it.

PETER. Casual and trendy clothes are best.

CALVIN. Simple button-down shirts and nice jeans make up most of Calvin's wardrobe. A sweater for date night.

DOUGLAS. Preppy casual. On Halloween, he dresses as an investigator but wears a bowler hat instead of the traditional deerstalker cap. Whenever the weather calls for it (and especially on Halloween), Douglas wears an old red scarf.

DOTTY. Dotty doesn't leave the house unless she's put together.

CASSIE. Yoga pants, athletic shirts, and comfortable slip-on shoes. She always wears red lipstick or lip tint.